KU-193-649

IN SEARCH OF SUNSHINE

ELSIE MILLIGAN

LONDON
PICKERING & INGLIS LTD
1964

PICKERING & INGLIS LTD.
29 Ludgate Hill, London, E.C.4
229 Bothwell Street, Glasgow, C.2
Home Evangel Books Ltd., 25 Hobson Avenue, Toronto, 16

Made and Printed in Great Britain

CONTENTS

CHAPTER I

BIRTHDAY IN BED

"OH, Doctor, please let me get up for my birthday party, please," begged Tricia.

The tall Scots doctor smiled down at the flushed anxious face of his young patient and said, "No, my lassie, I'm afraid it's birthday in bed for you this year, but, never mind, I'm sure you will have a lovely party all the same. Who knows—I might come to it myself, if you ask me!"

"Oh, yes, doctor, please do come, we'd love you to," said Tricia.

Timothy and Tricia Bevan were twins and the next day they were going to be eleven. They were not so much like each other as twins usually are, for Timothy was tall and had brown eyes and curly brown hair, whereas Tricia was two inches shorter and had hazel eyes and her hair was straight and a lighter brown.

Of course Tricia's full name was Patricia, but when she was very small she had called herself Tricia, so everyone else called her that too. She did not like to be called Pat or Patty or even Patricia—just Tricia.

Timothy, on the other hand, liked to be called by his full name. Woe betide anyone who called him Tim or Timmy! Nothing but the full Timothy would do for him!

Although they were not so much alike to look at, they were true twins at heart and devoted to each other. They had a young sister named Melanie, and a still younger brother named Brian, of whom they were very fond, but their love for each other was something apart. And even though they had reached an age when Timothy had some boy friends of his own and Tricia had some girl friends of her own, yet they remained as devoted as ever to each other. And now that poor Tricia was ill in bed and not allowed up even for their birthday, Timothy was as disappointed and upset about it as she was.

The doctor followed Mrs. Bevan downstairs into the sitting-room. "It's too bad," he said, "about Tricia's party, but really it would be dangerous to let her up while she is still running a temperature, though it is not high now. Also it's important for her to remain in one room with an even temperature until this bronchial trouble clears up."

"Yes, doctor, I quite understand," said Tricia's mother, "and we must just try to make up to her for her disappointment. If you could spare a few minutes to look in at the party, that would be a big help."

"I'll certainly do my best, Mrs. Bevan. This last attack has been very deep-seated, and has taken much longer to clear up than I expected," said the doctor.

"Yes," agreed Mrs. Bevan. "If we had thought it would have lasted so long, we would have postponed the party, but it's nearly three weeks now since she went to bed, and I thought she would surely be better by now."

"There is no doubt," the doctor went on, "that Tricia has a definite chest weakness—no actual disease—but a weakness left over from that bad go of double pneumonia which she had when she was four. However, I hope she will get on top of it soon. What she really needs," he added, "is sunshine—to live in a warm sunny climate for a while."

As he spoke, the doctor looked out of the window at the grey gloomy sky, and thought of the poor summer they had had in England that year, and the cold wind which had ushered in the autumn.

"You mean some place like the south of France, doctor," said Mrs. Bevan sadly, "but that, of course, would be out of the question for us."

"Of course," the doctor agreed, "so we must just do our best without it. Goodbye, Mrs. Bevan, and I will pop in to the party tomorrow if at all possible."

The next day turned out to be fine and all the morning great preparations went on for the party. Tricia, after one little weep over her disappointment, had cheered up like a sensible girl and was looking forward to her share of the party. For her mother had promised that the guests should all come in to see her, two at a time, and that the birthday cake should be brought in for her to blow out her half of the candles. She was dressed in a lovely new blue dressing-gown which had been her mother's birthday present to her, and a wide blue ribbon to match on her hair.

Punctually at three o'clock the guests started to arrive. There were eight of them altogether, four boys and four girls, and each of them brought a small present for the twins, some were joint ones for them both, like games, and some were separate ones for each of them. It was very exciting opening the parcels and seeing what each contained.

The guests played some games until teatime, and when they were called into the dining-room for tea, there were loud Oooos and Aaaas at the sight of the table. How pretty it looked with flowers and decorations, apart altogether from the nice things to eat! Mrs. Bevan had been busy indeed, and there were all sorts of nice little cakes with coloured icing on top, and jam tarts and scones and pancakes, as well as jellies in small individual dishes, some red, some yellow, and some green, each with a big dollop of cream on the top. Serviettes with entertaining pictures were beside each plate and added to the gaiety of the whole scene.

Of course, the most exciting thing of all on the table was the birthday cake which Mrs. Bevan had made and iced herself. It was beautifully done and had the names

'Tricia' and 'Timothy' written in pink icing. It was a big cake and there were twenty-two candles on it, eleven on one half of it, and eleven on the other half.

Tricia's special friend Pamela was allowed to have tea in the bedroom with Tricia, and for them Mrs. Bevan had prepared a large tray upon which were some of all the goodies upon the table at the party. It was a real party tray, and the two girls enjoyed their birthday tea just as much as those at the party proper, though they didn't make nearly as much noise over it as the dining-room party did.

At last the great moment arrived and the birthday cake was carried carefully upstairs for Tricia to see and to blow out her eleven candles. She and Pamela were given the first two slices of the cake. Timothy had gone upstairs with the cake and as he watched Tricia blowing out her candles, he said, "This is the last time we will have candles on our birthday cake because next birthday we shall be twelve and too big for things like that."

"Well," Tricia said, "in that case we must make the most of the candles this year. It's fun blowing them out but I haven't got much puff." Indeed, her attempts to blow out the candles had brought on such a bad fit of coughing that her mother was quite alarmed, and Timothy had to finish the job for her.

After tea there were more party games and in the middle of the fun in came Dr. Macduff. Several of the children knew him and he was given a great welcome and a large slice of birthday cake. After a little while he went up to see Tricia. This made her very happy, especially when he handed her a small parcel saying, "Here's my birthday offering."

"Oh, thank you, doctor," said Tricia, "I wonder what it is." As she spoke, she was feeling the packet with practised fingers trying to guess what it was. "It's a book," she announced.

"Open it," commanded the doctor, "and see which one," Tricia opened it, and to her joy, she found that it was a book all about birds. It had lovely coloured pictures of all the different sorts of birds that are found in Britain and abroad.

"Oh, how lovely!" said Tricia, "but, doctor, how did you know that I was keen on birds."

"Ah," said the doctor, "a little bird told me!" Everyone laughed, and soon afterwards, the doctor had to hurry away. All agreed that it had been a very nice party, and although she was very tired when it was all over, Tricia said, "I wouldn't have thought that I could enjoy a birthday in bed so much."

Later on when the other children were all in bed and Tricia had been tucked up after having a sedative to calm her down after all the excitement, Mr. and Mrs. Bevan sat in the sitting-room and talked.

"Well," said Mr. Bevan, "so the twins are eleven! They are growing up very fast."

"Yes," said Mrs. Bevan, "and I'm worried that Tricia is still so delicate. I hoped that by now, she would have grown out of this chest weakness. The doctor says there is no disease, just a weakness which makes her prone to these bronchial attacks. He says that she needs sunshine and a warm climate for a while."

"We haven't had much sunshine this summer," said Mr. Bevan, "and now the winter is before us. I sometimes wonder whether we ought not to move down to the south of England for her sake, it would be a bit warmer there."

"And to think that in Betty's letter last week, they were complaining about too much heat in South Africa!" said Mrs. Bevan.

'Betty' was Mrs. Bevan's sister Elizabeth de Villiers who had married a South African and gone to live in Johannesburg.

Mr. and Mrs. Bevan talked over the problem of Tricia's delicate health, and before they went to bed, they had prayer together about Tricia and all their children. Yes, they knew where to take their troubles. Both of them knew God as their loving Heavenly Father in whom they trusted, and they had taught their children to trust in Him too.

"Guide us, loving Father," Mr. Bevan prayed, "as to the best treatment for Tricia that she may get strong and well again, and bless us all. For Christ's sake. Amen."

CHAPTER II

THE INVITATION

TRICIA was convalescent now. She was up and dressed, but not yet allowed to go out because there was still a cold wind blowing. She was seated at the dining-room table writing letters.

Unlike most children, Tricia really liked writing letters. She had a flair for letter-writing, and did not look upon it as a dreadful bore to have to write thank you letters for her birthday presents as Timothy did. She was writing now to her aunt who lived in South Africa. She wrote,

"Dear Auntie Betty,

"Thank you so much for the nice long letter you wrote me and the postal order for my birthday present. Timothy thanks you for his, too, and says that he will write to you himself soon. I am going to put my money towards getting a tennis racquet as I'm learning to play tennis at school now.

Timothy and I had a very happy birthday and a lovely party, but unfortunately I was in bed. I had been in bed for three weeks with bronchitis and it wasn't better when my birthday arrived.

But I am much better now and up and about, but the doctor won't let me go out yet because it is cold and windy. Timothy heard our doctor tell Mummy that what I need is 'sunshine'. I was thinking how nice it would be if you could send me some 'sunshine' from South Africa where you seem to have such a lot of it.

It's a pity that I've had to miss so much school, though Mummy makes me do some lessons at home. My favourite subjects are History and English Literature.

I hope that you and Uncle Dennis are well and also Georgina. Please send me a snapshot of you all when you have one taken, I'm sure Georgina has grown a lot since the last one you sent.

Mummy and Daddy send their love to you, and so do Timothy and I. Brian is three now and is full of mischief. Melanie is at school and so far she loves it, but she won't like it so much later on when she gets hard lessons to do, I am sure.

Thank you again for my birthday present, and please write to me again, Auntie, when you get time as I love getting letters from you.

Lots of love from

Tricia."

"There Mummy," said Tricia, "that's Auntie Betty's letter finished, have you got a stamp for me, I've addressed the envelope?"

"Yes," replied her mother, "there is one in my desk, and Timothy can run to the post with it when he comes in from school. I think we'll send it airmail, and I will put in a little note for Auntie too."

So off went Tricia's letter to Johannesburg in South Africa and when it arrived there, it was such a hot day that Auntie Betty was sitting out on the stoep (verandah) when the postman came, and instead of putting it into the letter-box, he handed it to her.

"Bring me my glasses, please," she called to her own small daughter who had just come home from school. "It's a letter from England, from Auntie Jenny, I expect," she said as she took the glasses and opened the letter.

"Oh, it's from Tricia," she exclaimed, "or most of it, there is just a short note from Auntie." She started to read the letter and Georgina ran into the house to get a cold drink for it was so hot and she was thirsty.

Mrs. De Villiers read Tricia's letter through.

"Poor child!" she thought, as she read of the bad

attack of bronchitis. She smiled as she read the bit about wishing she could send some of South Africa's sunshine over to them in England. "I wish indeed that I could," she thought.

Then as she sat there thinking, suddenly an idea came to her; it was such a startling idea that it rather took her breath away, but the more she thought about it, the more she liked it. If the mountain could not go to Mahomet why not bring Mahomet to the mountain? In other words—she could not send the South African sunshine to Tricia, but why not invite Tricia to come out to South Africa and spend a year or at least a few months with them in Johannesburg! She could hardly wait till Georgina was in bed that evening to discuss the matter with her husband. She did not want her daughter to hear of it yet in case nothing came of the idea.

"I think it's a grand idea," said her husband, when he heard of it, "it's a wonder we have not thought of it before. This climate will fix Tricia's chest trouble I'm sure. The sooner she comes the better."

"Oh, but her parents may not be willing to part with her," said Auntie Betty, "or the child may not want to come. We mustn't count on it. Then there's Timothy—Tricia may not want to be parted from her twin for so long. But a short visit won't have the same effect."

"Invite Timothy too," said her husband, "and tell Jenny that Tricia will really need a year out here to put her right."

So, the very next day a letter from Auntie Betty soared up into the sky, in the Boeing plane which carried the mail, and four days later it fell through the letter-box in the front door of the Bevan's home in Liverpool.

By this time Tricia was well enough to go back to school, so her mother was alone in the house when the letter arrived. She read it while she was drinking her mid-morning cup of coffee, and what a surprise she had! She was so startled by the invitation in the letter, that she quite forgot a batch of scones which was in the oven, and they were baked to a cinder before the burning smell reminded her about them.

Her first thought when she had read the letter was "Oh, it's very, very kind of Betty to invite the twins, but we couldn't possibly be parted from them for a whole year." But as the afternoon wore on, other thoughts came to her. There was no doubt that the South African climate would be wonderful for Tricia, and might cure her altogether of the chest weakness that she had. Then, too, might it not be that this letter was the answer to their fervent prayers that the Lord would guide them how to help Tricia in the matter of her health. By the time that her husband came home from work that evening, she was feeling torn in two, and was longing to discuss it with him. He was so sane and wise, and would know the right thing to do.

"Mother," said Daddy, at supper time that evening, "you forgot to put any salt in the potatoes."

"Oh, dear," said Mother, "I'm so sorry I'm afraid I must have been thinking of something else at the time."

"What were you thinking of, Mummy?" asked Timothy.

"Oh, nothing special," replied his Mother hastily, "or rather," she added, "it was something special, but I can't tell you about it now."

Her family looked at her in surprise and with interest.

"Is it a secret, Mummy?" asked Tricia.

"Yes," said her mother, "for the present it is."

"When can we know about it?" asked Timothy.

But now Daddy came to the rescue.

"No more questions," he said, "eat up your supper. When Mummy is ready to let us know the secret, she will tell us and until then, you must just possess your souls in patience.

"Do you know what it is Daddy?" asked Timothy.

"What did I say about no more questions," said his father. So the children had to be content to wait. After supper they did their homework, then sat by the fire reading until bedtime. It was not until they were safely in bed that Mrs. Bevan produced the letter from Johannesburg and gave it to her husband to read. As he did so she watched his face to see how he would react to the startling invitation. To her surprise he was delighted.

"Why," he said, "this is wonderful—it's the very thing! It'll probably set Tricia up in health altogether. The South African climate is marvellous for weak chests, and how very kind of Betty and Dennis to offer to have Tricia for a whole year. I'm sure we can trust her to them—you see what she says about all the care they'll take of her, and I'm sure they will, too. Aren't you glad about it?"

"I . . . I don't know," said Mrs. Bevan a little shakily, "it's wonderful of them, I agree, and I expect it would be the very thing, as you say, for Tricia, but what about us being parted from her for a whole year? What shall we do without her?"

"Yes, of course," said Mr, Bevan, slightly taken aback. Then he went on, "Of course we shall miss them dreadfu'ly, but surely we can put up with that if it means the child's health being restored."

"You said 'them'," said Mrs. Bevan. "Do you think that Timothy must go too?"

"Certainly!" said her husband. "If Tricia goes, Timothy goes too. We couldn't send a child like Tricia to a strange land on her own, but with Timothy she will be all right. I don't think it would be wise to separate them just now."

"I agree with you there," said Mrs. Bevan, after a minute, "and I think it might reconcile Tricia to the idea of going if Timothy goes too."

"Why, do you think she won't want to go? asked her

husband. "I should have thought that any child would jump at the idea of going to South Africa for a long visit."

"But Tricia is a shy little thing," said her mother, "and, after all, she has never been away from me in her life except when she was in hospital. Still, the more I think about it, the more I feel that she ought to go, that it is too good a chance to miss. As you say, her health should come before any other considerations."

"To me," said Mr. Bevan, "it seems the most wonderful answer to prayer. We prayed for guidance to know what to do for Tricia to get her well and strong, and here it is."

Mrs. Bevan smiled at her husband and said, "Yes, I think you are right. Here it is! I'm afraid I was just being selfish in thinking of my own feelings."

"Not selfish, dear," said her husband, " just natural and motherly. I tell you what," he added, "let's go round and see Dr. Macduff and hear what he has to say."

So round they went to their family doctor, and there was no doubt about what he thought.

"It's a marvellous chance," he cried delightedly, "jump at it. Write and accept the invitation by return of post. You can't get that child into the sunshine of South Africa too soon."

On the way back Mr. Bevan said, "Well, Mother, I think that settles it, don't you?"

"Yes," Mrs. Bevan agreed," but how are we going to pay their fares."

"They'll have to fly," said Mr. Bevan. "It's the only way when they are on their own. I wish you could have gone, too, the trip would have done you good, but there are the two little ones."

"Not to mention you, my Big One," said his wife laughing.

"Oh, I could look after myself," said Mr. Bevan, "but all the same I'm glad I shan't have to. Well, about the fares, I'll just have to take the money we are saving up for a car. This is more important. I'll get busy right away tomorrow enquiring about air passages. You see, we can take them to London and put them on the plane in charge of the air hostess one day and they will land in South Africa the next day and be met at the airport by their auntie and uncle. It's wonderful when you think of it."

"Yes," Mrs. Bevan agreed, "we couldn't send them by boat unless we knew someone reliable with whom they could travel."

"And with the winter almost here, the sooner Tricia is out of this climate the better. How long do you need to get them ready to go?" asked Mr. Bevan.

"About a fortnight," said Mrs. Bevan, "and that will give me a little time to get used to the idea."

At prayers that night, Tricia's parents thanked God for this wonderful answer to their request, and asked for His blessing on the plan as they proceeded to carry it out.

CHAPTER III

OFF TO SOUTH AFRICA

WHEN Mrs. Bevan told Tricia about her aunt's invitation, she was thrilled at first.

"And you will come too, Mummy, won't you?" she said.

"No, darling," said her mother, "how could I leave the little ones and Daddy. Who would look after them?"

"But can't we all go together, Mummy?" asked Tricia.

"Daddy couldn't leave his work," Mummy explained, "and besides, it would cost far too much money for us all to go. Anyway, Aunt Betty hasn't invited us all to go, she has asked only you and Timothy to go and stay with her for a long visit, and I think it is very, very kind of her, don't you?"

"Yes, Mummy, I do," said Tricia, "and I should love to go, but I don't want to leave you. I'd rather stay at home if you can't come."

"I know how you feel, darling," said her mummy, "and I feel sad too at the thought of being parted from you, but, you see, the whole plan is so that you can enjoy the sunshine and warm climate of South Africa and that you will become quite strong and well again instead of always having these awful attacks of bronchitis. You want to get well and strong like Timothy, don't you?"

"Yes, I do," said Tricia fervently, "but I don't want to leave you."

Just then they heard Timothy coming in at the front gate on his way home from school.

"I'm sure Timothy will be thrilled when he hears about it," said Mrs. Bevan.

"Oh, Mummy, please let me tell him," said Tricia urgently.

"I know a secret," she teased her brother as he came

in to the kitchen where she and her mother had been talking.

"I know a secret that you don't know, Timothy," Tricia repeated.

"Tell me," said Timothy coming over to her, "tell me quick."

"We're going out to South Africa to stay with Auntie Betty, you and me," Tricia announced triumphantly.

"Go on," said Timothy, unbelievingly, "you don't expect me to believe that, do you."

"But it's true, Timothy," said his sister who was enjoying herself hugely, "you and me are going all by ourselves on an aeroplane to Johannesburg."

Tricia was so excited by now that she couldn't worry about grammar.

Timothy's face was a study. First a look of thrilled excitement, then doubt, for surely this was too good to be true.

"You tell him, Mummy," said Tricia in the end. "Get Auntie's letter and show him."

When this was done and Timothy was finally convinced that he wasn't being had on, his joy knew no bounds. He was wild with delight. He had no qualms about parting from the rest of the family. It was enough for him that he was included in the invitation. He went whooping round the house with excitement, then dashed off down the road to tell his chum.

Tricia caught some of the excitement from him and, much to her mother's relief, she accepted the idea of going without further protest.

"I'm going to tell Dr. Macduff about it," Tricia told her mother. "Won't he be surprised!"

"He knows already," said her mother, "in fact it was he who first suggested to us that it would help you very much if you could live for a time in a warm, sunny climate. He is very pleased about it."

"Then who told Auntie Betty?" asked Tricia.

"No-one told her," said Mummy, "but I think that it was something that you said in your letter to her that first gave her the idea."

"I know," said Tricia, "I said that I wished that she could send us some of their lovely sunshine."

"That must have been it," said Mummy.

"I guess it was God who put the idea into Auntie Betty's head," said Timothy solemnly.

"You're quite right, son," said his mother, "Daddy and I had been praying about it and asking God to show us what to do to make Tricia stronger. So when Auntie's letter came, it was a great answer to our prayers."

"Well, it was a jolly good idea," said Timothy, "and when I say my prayers tonight, I'm going to say 'Thank you' to Him."

"So shall I," said Tricia, not to be outdone by her brother.

What a hectic time the twins and their mother had in the days that followed! There was so much to do in preparation for their departure two weeks later. Tricia accompanied her mother to town to buy material for the making of a number of summer frocks. What fun it was choosing the patterns and the materials! Then Mrs. Bevan set to work and spent hours dressmaking, with Tricia hovering round and helping in many little ways. Timothy, too, had to be taken shopping to get khaki shorts and new shirts and other things. Daddy had to draw money from the Savings Bank for all these things as well as for air fares. He shook his head as the money vanished on one thing and another. "Did ever any man have such expensive twins as I've got?" he asked the children, teasing them. But for them it was all great fun and so exciting that Mummy had to try all the time to keep Tricia from getting over-tired, or from taking cold.

The days flew by at a great rate and the last Sunday

came. They all went to church on the Sunday morning as usual and the children went to Sunday School in the afternoon. Here the Superintendent told the whole School that Tricia and Timothy were going out to South Africa, leaving by air on the following Wednesday. Every eye in Sunday School was turned to look at the twins and they felt very important. Then the Superintendent prayed specially for them, that God would take care of them and give them a safe journey to Africa and a happy time there.

On Monday the actual packing began. Each of the twins had a brand new suitcase and had to watch as Mummy packed their things, so that they would know where to find them when they arrived in Africa. The trouble was that both Tricia and Timothy wanted to take all sorts of treasures and games with them and the suitcases were full before half of their clothes were packed.

"No," said Mummy, "this won't do at all. We must pack the clothes and necessary things first, then if there is any room over, you may put your other things in."

"But can't we take another suitcase, Mummy?" Tricia asked.

"No," her mother explained, "you see each passenger on the plane is only allowed to take forty-four pounds of luggage, and one suitcase will weigh that."

So, reluctantly, Tricia had to leave all her dolls at home except her one special favourite, and Timothy had to say 'Goodbye' for the time being to most of his treasures. They each took a few favourite books, for they were both fond of reading.

What a job it was trying to get everything in to the suitcases, and trying to get the lids shut! But Mother managed it at last. To their great joy, the children were each given a blue Airways bag to carry with them on the journey. All sorts of oddments found their way into these bags and they were soon bulging.

The last day came and the friend who was going to stay in the house and look after Melanie and Brian while Mr. and Mrs. Bevan took the twins to London, arrived to take over.

Long before the taxi came which was to take them to the station at Liverpool, Timothy was rushing out every other minute to look for it. Goodbyes were said to the little ones who wondered what all the commotion was about, then they were enticed into a neighbour's house before the actual departure took place.

At Liverpool station, Tricia was terrified by all the noise and bustle and clung closely to her mother, but Timothy was in his element watching the powerful train engines which came whistling into the station, or puffed their way out of it. To the children the train journey to London was a treat. Timothy enjoyed every minute of it, especially the dinner which they had in the dining-saloon.

"It's fun to eat our dinner with everything on the table moving about," Timothy declared, as the train swayed and rattled along.

After dinner Tricia fell asleep for she was tired out with so much excitement. It was a good thing that she had a nice long sleep for more excitement than ever awaited them when they arrived in London.

From the big station there, they took a taxi out to the London Airport. Here Timothy's excitement exceeded all bounds as, from the balcony where they were sitting, they saw the big planes coming down to land, and others rising up and setting out on the flights to far-away lands. Tricia was thrilled to watch them, too, but she was feeling a little bit nervous at the thought of going on one of them herself.

Before they had left home Daddy had called the children together and with Mummy, too, had prayed to God to give the twins a safe journey to Africa. Then he had given their tickets and other papers to Timothy and helped him to put them safely in the lovely new wallet which had been his Daddy's parting present to him.

"You see," Daddy had told him, "you're the man of the party and you must take care of Tricia, and give these papers to Uncle Dennis when you arrive in Johannesburg."

This made Timothy feel very important and grown up.

Just then a voice came over the loud speaker saying, "Will all the passengers for Flight No. 664 for Johannesburg go to the bus which will take them out to the plane."

"That's us," said Timothy jumping up excitedly.

"Yes," said Daddy, "that's you. Come we will take you to the Air Hostess who is going to take care of you on the journey." They went with a whole stream of other passengers to a gateway where an official was checking the tickets. Beside him stood a tall young lady in a very smart blue uniform. Daddy introduced the children to her.

"This is Tricia," he said, "and this is Timothy, they are twins."

"Oh, how interesting!" said the Air Hostess, and she smiled at the children in such a friendly way that they took an instant liking to her.

Then came the 'Goodbyes', but mercifully they had to be brief as the Air Hostess was waiting to escort the children to the bus that would take them out to the plane. Tricia clung desperately to her mother at the last and even Timothy felt a strange feeling in his throat and had to swallow very hard.

"Don't worry about Tricia," he said to his parents, "I will take care of her," and as he spoke, he threw out his chest and felt very grown up.

"God bless you, darlings," said Mummy, "and keep you safe, and bring you back to us strong and well."

"Goodbye, Chicks, be good and do what Auntie and Uncle tell you," said their father.

A last bear hug from each of them and they were off with the Air Hostess to the waiting bus, that took them out to the plane.

"It's a Comet, isn't it?" Timothy asked the Air Hostess.

"Yes, it's a Comet 3," she replied.

"It's super!" cried Timothy, gazing with interest at the great silver coloured aeroplane which was standing there waiting to swallow them up along with about fifty other passengers.

Even Tricia looked with interest at the giant plane and said, "Oh, dear, how can such a big heavy thing ever get up into the air?"

The Air Hostess laughed and said, "It is wonderful, isn't it, but the big powerful engines won't have any difficulty about that; you'll see just now. Up you go," said the Air Hostess, when they reached the foot of the gangway.

Timothy took Tricia's hand and helped her up the steps of the gangway. At the top they turned and waved just in case Mother and Father could see them, and this made Tricia weep afresh. However, the kind Hostess soon had her seated in a comfy armchair seat about halfway down the plane with Timothy next to her in the seat by the window. A leather belt from the seat was fastened round them and soon, when all the passengers were in, the door was shut. Then the engines were started one after the other, Timothy craning his neck eagerly to see each one as it fired, building up power, slowly at first, then faster and faster, to a shrill pitch.

A few minutes later Timothy said excitedly, "We're airborne, look, the ground's going away from us."

"I don't want to look," said Tricia, who was a bit nervous.

"No" said the Hostess coming along at that moment, "of course you don't want to look out of the window, but here are some interesting magazines for you to look at, and just now I shall be bringing you a Coca-Cola to drink."

And from the balcony Mother and Father watched as the plane containing their Tricia and Timothy rose into the air like a great big silvery bird. It almost seemed to them as though the wings of it flapped as it turned and headed south. The twins were on their way to South Africa!

CHAPTER IV

FLYING IS FUN

ON that same day when the Comet left London Airport with Timothy and Tricia on board, they were not the only children that were excited. Away in South Africa, in Johannesburg, there was a very excited girl of ten-years-old awaiting their arrival. This was their cousin Georgina, who was tremendously thrilled that her cousins from England, whom she had never seen, were coming out to stay for a long visit. She herself was an only child, and although she had friends to play with, she was sometimes lonely at home. But now Tricia and Timothy would actually be staying in her home, and Tricia would be sharing her bedroom. No wonder that she skipped joyfully around the house that day, helping her mother in the preparations which she was making for the visitors.

First of all an extra bed was put up in Georgina's room. Then her mother said, "We must give Tricia two of these drawers in the chest of drawers to keep her things in, and half of the space in the wardrobe. An extra chair was brought in and put beside Tricia's bed. Soon the room was all ready and looked so nice with it's pale green furniture, and two or three gay pictures on the walls.

"What about some flowers, Mummy?" said Georgina. "Shall I pick some from the garden? I could put them in the little green vase."

"That's a lovely idea," agreed her mother, "but I would wait and do them tomorrow morning if I were you, then they will be nice and fresh when Tricia comes. The plane doesn't get here till about half past two in the afternoon, so you will have plenty of time."

"Can I go to the airport with you and Daddy to meet them?" asked Georgina.

"Of course you can, dear," replied her mother. "We will have to leave here soon after lunch. And now let us go and get Timothy's room ready for him."

That didn't take long. It was a small room at the end of the verandah. They made up the bed and Georgina dusted the room nicely, and it was soon ready.

"Now Gina," said her mother, "we'll go and start the baking I think." Off they went to the kitchen, which was a nice roomy, cheerful one and had a big window which looked out on to the garden at the back. Under the window was a long seat on which Gina loved to sit and watch her mother when she was baking.

"What are you going to make, Mummy?" she asked now.

"I'm going to make some gingerbread and cookies, and an apple-tart, and perhaps some of those new biscuits if we have time," said her mother.

"Those were lovely biscuits," said Georgina, "I'm sure the twins will like them."

So the day of getting ready passed happily by, and Georgina's last thought before she went to sleep that night was, "Tomorrow they'll be here."

* * * *

Meantime the Comet was speeding through the air at a great speed. It was so steady that the people inside it could hardly believe that they were flying. Tricia didn't feel at all happy at first, it was all so strange and she was nervous. Although she would not look out of the window herself, Timothy kept her well posted as to all that there was to be seen.

"The houses look tiny now," he told her, "just like dolls' houses." Then the plane rose so high that nothing could be seen but clouds billowing about underneath.

As suppertime drew near, the children watched with

interest as the stewards went round with little blue trays. Each passenger had his or her supper on one of these trays. By the time that this meal was over it was quite dark outside and the lights were all on in the plane.

"We shall soon be landing at Rome to refuel and after that you will be able to settle down to sleep for the night," the Air Hostess told them.

"Rome!" exclaimed Timothy, "how exciting! That means that we shall be in Italy. What a pity we shan't be able to see it in the dark!"

At the airport in Rome they were regaled with coffee and biscuits. Timothy watched the re-fuelling of the plane with interest. Then they climbed into it again and away they flew into the night.

The Air Hostess came and let back the seats of the children so that they could lie back comfortably. They each had a pillow and were tucked up with a blanket so that it was nearly as good as being in bed. The lights were lowered and most of the passengers settled down to go to sleep, though some kept on reading by the light of the small reading lamp above each seat.

Tricia was very tired, but she couldn't go to sleep. Home-sickness overcame her and the tears began to trickle down her face. She buried her face in her pillow and hoped that no-one would know that she was crying. But Timothy knew. He wasn't scornful though like he sometimes was when Tricia cried. He slipped his hand under the blanket and gave her hand a squeeze.

"Don't cry, Tricia," he whispered, "I'm here and I'll take care of you."

"I know," sobbed Tricia, "but I want Mummy."

His silent sympathy helped and soon Tricia stopped crying.

"Have you said your prayers?" asked Timothy.

"No," whispered Tricia, "I can't say them on the plane, and anyway I can't kneel down."

"God won't mind about that," said Timothy, "you can just say them in your heart and He can hear, and it'll make you feel better."

And sure enough Tricia did feel better after she had whispered her prayers to Jesus and unburdened her heavy little heart, and almost at once she fell asleep.

When they woke in the morning the sun was shining brightly into the plane and the children wondered for a minute wherever they were.

They were in Kenya and were just about to land at Nairobi Airport. Out they had to get now and soon the twins found themselves in the airport restaurant doing justice to the good breakfast which was set before them. Tricia had not been able to eat much supper the night before, so she was quite hungry now. As for Timothy he was always hungry when mealtimes came round, or there was something radically wrong with him if he wasn't.

Soon after they took off from Nairobi, one of the pilots came and told the children to look out of the window and they might see some wild animals. They peered eagerly down and saw the forests and plains of Kenya below them, but they could not spot any elephants or other animals.

"Sometimes we do see them," the pilot told them, "but not this time evidently." Soon they were up too high again to see anything but the clouds rolling in fleecy billows beneath them.

Tricia was very interested in a baby who was travelling on the plane. She went along to the front to see him in the small sort of pen in which he was put when he wasn't in his cot, and she sat beside him and played with him for quite a while. He was delighted with her attentions and gave her the most enchanting smiles and gurgles.

The next excitement was when the plane came down at Salisbury and the passengers all had coffee or tea at the airport, all except Tricia and Timothy who had Coca-Colas instead.

When they were back on the plane once more, Timothy said to Tricia, "The next time the plane comes down we shall be there. I'd like to go on flying for another day or two—flying's fun."

"Yes, it is," agreed Tricia, "but all the same I've had quite enough, and I shall be glad to arrive. I wonder if Auntie and Uncle and Georgina will all be at the airport to meet us."

"The airport at Johannesburg is called Jan Smuts Airport after General Smuts, the pilot told me," said Timothy.

It was soon after two o'clock that the now familiar sign came on in lights, 'Fasten your safety-belts'.

"That means that we're going down to land," said Timothy excitedly.

"I don't like the feeling when the plane is coming down," said Tricia, "it makes me feel funny inside."

Soon there was a gentle bump.

"We've touched down," shouted Timothy.

Everybody in the plane was gathering up their belongings and getting ready for the arrival. Soon they could see crowds of people standing on the long balcony at the airport building. The children looked at the crowd of waiting people.

"I wonder which of them is Auntie Betty and Uncle Dennis," said Tricia.

They were soon to know.

CHAPTER V

ARRIVED

GEORGINA and her mother and father stood on the balcony of Jan Smuts Airport, eagerly scanning the sky for the first glimpse of the Comet which was bringing the twins out to them.

Many other people were waiting there with them. Suddenly a man said, "There it is!" and he pointed away to the north, and there sure enough a tiny black speck could be seen. Everyone turned to look where he was pointing.

"I see it," cried Georgina, jumping up and down with excitement. Quickly now the Comet came in, the sun glinting on her as she got larger and larger. Then graceful as a bird she swooped down towards the far runway, and soon she was taxi-ing along the ground. Eagerly Georgina watched as the man went out on to the tarmac and raised his hands to guide her into position.

"We had better go downstairs now," Georgina's father said, "and be ready to take over the twins from the Air Hostess." They hurried down and got as near to the entrance as possible. There was the Comet standing still now and looking huge. Now the door was thrown open and people started to come out. One after another they came, some of them waving to friends and relations in the waiting crowd, but no sign of the twins. Georgina began to get anxious, "Perhaps they haven't come," she wailed.

"I know what's happened," said her Daddy, "I expect that the Air Hostess will bring them out last of all after the other passengers are all out."

And that is just what happened. They saw the trim figure of a smart young lady in uniform come out behind all the other plane passengers, and with her were a boy and a girl. Gina's father spoke to the official standing at the entrance, and got permission to go out and meet them.

"Are these Timothy and Tricia Bevan?" he asked, "I am their uncle."

"Oh, good!" said the Air Hostess, "then I can hand them safely over to you. Will you go with them to the Customs and Immigration? This young man has all the necessary papers and the ticket for the luggage."

Timothy came forward now and shook hands with his uncle, and Tricia came more shyly behind to receive a welcoming kiss from this great big man who was her new uncle.

"Thank you for looking after them," said Uncle Dennis to the Air Hostess.

"It was a pleasure," she said, "they were very good—no trouble at all."

The twins then said 'Goodbye' to her, and they felt that they were leaving a real friend.

They hurried along to the Customs which was downstairs in the basement of the Airport. There everything went through smoothly and quickly and up the stairs they came to find Aunt Betty and Georgina waiting there to meet them. Uncle Dennis made the introductions.

"Welcome to South Africa," said their aunt as she gave them such a warm welcoming kiss that even shy Tricia felt at home with her. There was no shyness about Timothy, however, and he greeted them all heartily and started right in telling them about their flight.

"It was super," he said, "I could have gone on flying for ever."

"Come now," said his uncle, "and help me to pick out your suitcases from this lot that is coming up now."

As they went off to see about the luggage, Tricia and Georgina greeted each other shyly. Tricia kept a tight hold of Auntie Betty's arm. It was a comfort to her to find that her auntie was so like her Mummy, whose sister, of course, she was.

Soon the suitcases were located and carried out to the car by a fine big African porter. Then they all got into the car and set off on the big highway which led to the city of Johannesburg, for the airport was fifteen miles away from the city.

Auntie Betty and the two girls sat at the back and Timothy sat in the front seat beside his uncle. He had had a good look at the car before he got in and admired it very much.

"It's a big one, Uncle," he said, "what make is it?"

"It's a Plymouth," his uncle told him.

"I don't know this sort," said Timothy.

"No," said his uncle, "I expect British cars are used more in England. This is American." Timothy proceeded to chatter all the way in.

"The pilot let me go into the cockpit," he told them, "and showed me all the gadgets there. I'd like to be a pilot when I grow up."

"You've always said that you wanted to be a sailor before," said Tricia.

"Ah, but I hadn't been in a plane then," explained Timothy.

"Have you been on a boat?" asked Uncle Dennis, "a big one I mean?"

"I haven't sailed on one," admitted Timothy, "but I've been over some of them in the docks at Liverpool—Daddy took me."

"So now you want to be a pilot, eh?" said his uncle, "well, I expect your ambitions will change a few times yet before you are old enough to decide."

"And how did you enjoy the journey in the Comet, Tricia? asked her aunt.

"I was a bit nervous at first," Tricia admitted, "but afterwards it was nice, but I was glad to get here."

"And we're so glad, too, to have you," said Auntie Betty, "and we hope you are soon going to lose your cough and get quite strong and well here in our lovely sunshine."

"The sun is hot here," remarked Timothy, "we won't need to wear our coats much."

"No, you will only need summer clothes most of the time," said her aunt.

"I've written down in my book all the names of the places where our plane came down," Timothy went on, determined not to be side-tracked from his account of the flight, "and of the countries that we flew over, the pilot told me their names—it was very interesting, because we've learnt about them at school in geography. But we didn't see much of them because we were too high up and the clouds were in between."

He paused to look eagerly round at the country through which they were passing and at the approaches to the city.

"In a book at school," he said, "we read that Johannesburg was called 'The city of gold'."

"So you are looking round for the gold, are you?" laughed his uncle. "Well, it's here all right, but it's thousands of feet down in the earth beneath us. There's the top of one of the gold mines," he said, pointing to a shafthead which they could see now, and that great mound near it is what we call a mine-dump. That's the stuff that's left after the gold has been taken out of it. The twins looked with interest at the huge mine-dump which was soon to become such a familiar sight to them.

"It looks like gold," said Tricia. And indeed, the afternoon sun was shining on one side of the dump and did give it quite a golden look.

"We saw those mine-dumps from the plane just before we landed," said Timothy. "An old gentleman on the plane pointed them out to us, but they looked very small from the air, now they look so big."

"Here we are," said Uncle Dennis, as he turned the car off the main road into a quiet side turning. "We don't have to go right into the city, because we come to our suburb of Kensington first."

The car pulled in to the side of the road and stopped. The twins peered eagerly at the red brick square house at whose gate the car was now standing.

"This is our home," said Auntie Betty, "and here is Jeremiah coming to help us in with the luggage."

The children looked at the African boy who came out of the gate at that moment, his face one big beam of smiling welcome. He was followed by an excited terrier

"This is Patch, our dog," said Georgina. Patch cam running at the sound of his name and greeted all of the children with joyful little barks, and tried to jump up to lick Georgina's face.

"Down, Patch," she said. Then they all got out of the car and trooped into the house. The front door opened out of the wide shady verandah, and the house seemed dark and cool to the twins as they went in, after the hot sun outside.

"You take Tricia to your room, Gina," said her mother, "and I'll show Timothy where his little room is right here at the end of the stoep."

Timothy followed his aunt along. "What is a stoep?" he asked.

Auntie Betty laughed. "It's what you call a verandah in England but out here we call it a stoep. Here's your room and Jeremiah will bring your suitcase along. Can you unpack it later on, or shall I help you?"

"No, thank you, Auntie," said Timothy, "I can easily do it myself."

"We'll have tea as soon as the kettle boils," said Auntie Betty, and she went off to get it ready.

Later when they were having tea, their Aunt remarked, "It's amazing to think that you have come all that distance from England in less than twenty-four hours."

"The Comet is one of the fastest of all the jet planes," said Timothy.

"But was it only yesterday that we left home?" explained Tricia in surprise—"it seems a long time ago since we said 'Goodbye' to Mummy and Daddy."

Suddenly as she spoke, Tricia felt overwhelmed as she remembered the parting with her parents. She turned her head away quickly to hide the tears that sprang to her eyes. But her Aunt saw and with a comforting arm round her she drew Tricia close.

"Come," she said, "let's go and unpack your suitcase, and then Gina can take you round the garden. I think we'll have an early supper tonight and then you children must all get off to bed. Timothy and Tricia didn't get proper sleep last night."

"I'm not tired," said Timothy, "they tipped our seats back for beds last night, it was much more fun than ordinary beds."

"But not so restful, I'm sure," said his aunt. "Anyway, Tricia is very tired and can do with a long night."

Tricia found Auntie Betty very understanding and kind and she soon lost all her shyness with her.

"I'm glad you're like Mummy," she told her, "only she's not so tall as you."

"I think you are like your mother," her auntie told Tricia, "and I expect Timothy is like your father."

"Yes," everyone says so," said Tricia.

After the suitcase was unpacked Gina took Tricia out into the garden which was an interesting place with a small pond in which were gold-fish and lovely blue water-lilies. "There's a fountain in the middle," Gina explained to the twins, "and if you turn this tap on, the water comes shooting up."

Timothy ran to turn it on and had great fun watching and trying to regulate the spray of water.

"Why do you have wire over the pool?" asked Tricia.

"That's because some big white birds come sometimes and eat our goldfish. One day they ate them all, and Daddy had to get some new ones."

Tricia went into raptures over the canna lilies, pink ones and flame coloured ones which made the garden very gay. There were lovely roses too, and other flowers.

By supper time, Tricia and Gina were good friends, and Timothy had said "Hallo" to Jan Du Plessis, the boy next door, whom he had seen over the garden hedge.

CHAPTER VI

WRITING HOME

"WHAT a lovely morning!" cried Tricia the next morning when she woke up. The sunshine pouring in at the bedroom window was strong enough to make her blink even though it was only seven o'clock.

"It's nearly always a lovely morning here," Gina explained casually, "just sometimes in the summer it rains in the afternoon but not often."

The two girls got up and dressed and went out into the garden accompanied happily by Patch who fetched his old tennis ball and laid it hopefully at Gina's feet.

"He wants me to throw it for him," she explained to Tricia, and much to Patch's joy she threw it right down to the end of the garden. He retrieved it very quickly and brought it back, but this time he laid it at Tricia's feet.

Gina laughed, "That shows," she said, "that Patch has accepted you as one of the family. Now you must throw the ball for him."

Tricia threw the ball a few times and then they heard Gina's mother calling them in to breakfast.

"Timothy was already seated at the table when the girls went in.

"I walked down to the end of the road with Uncle Dennis," he told them.

"Yes," said Aunt Betty, "Uncle joins a friend of his there and they go in to work together. Next week they will go in Uncle's car."

"There's a lovely park at the other end of our road," said Gina, "it's called Rhodes Park. It's got a lake and a fountain and all sorts of interesting things."

"I was going to suggest," said her mother, "that you

should take your cousins to play there today, either this morning or this afternoon."

"Don't you have to go to school?" Timothy asked her.

"Yes, but it's holidays just now—half-term. We go back to school next Tuesday. Tricia can come to school with me if she likes, Mummy has arranged it with the Headmistress."

"That's right," said Auntie Betty. "We thought that you would soon get tired of doing nothing, so we spoke to the Headmistress and she has agreed to take Tricia for the time you are out here, that is if she well enough. How do you feel about it Tricia?"

"Yes, Auntie, I'd like to go with Gina. I'm quite well enough to go."

"You will be in a class above her, of course, but it is a nice school and I think you will like the other girls there."

"And how about me, Auntie?" asked Timothy.

"There is a Boys' School not far from here and Uncle has made an arrangement with the headmaster there, and he is willing for you to attend his school for the year that you are out here or it may be less, we shall see."

Timothy was not sure at first whether to be pleased or sorry about this. He had thought of this visit to South Africa as one long glorious holiday and the idea of school hadn't entered his mind. Still, school out here might be different from school at home in England—it might be rather fun after all.

"Jan Du Plessis, the boy next door goes to the same school," Gina volunteered to Timothy.

"Oh, good!" said Timothy, "I like the look of that boy, how old is he?"

"He's about twelve, I should think," said his Aunt, "he's a very nice boy, his family are Afrikaans."

"What does that mean?" asked Timothy.

"Well," Auntie Betty explained, "some of the white people in South Africa are descended from British people who came out from Britain and settled here many, many years ago. And others are descended from Dutch people who came out from Holland long ago. The latter are known as Afrikaans people, and very nice folk they are too. They speak the Afrikaans language, though they know English too. Both languages are official in this country—it's what we call a bilingual country. At school all children learn to speak both languages, which is quite right."

"As a matter of fact," she added, "in Jan's home next door they use English as their home language. I'm glad for your sake, Timothy, I expect you two boys will be great friends."

"And will Tricia and I have to learn Afrikaans when we go to school here?" asked Timothy.

"Well," replied his Aunt, "I don't suppose they'll make a point of it as you are only on a visit, but if I were you I would learn all you can while you are out here."

"Can you speak Afrikaans, Auntie?" asked Tricia.

"Yes," said her aunt, "I think everyone who lives in a bilingual country should try to understand and speak both languages. I'm afraid that Gina is not doing too well at it yet, but now that she is ten she must work hard and do better."

"Auntie," said Tricia, "I would like to write to Mummy this morning if I may."

"Of course, dear, that would be very nice, then Gina can take you to the park this afternoon. We'll have a quiet day today then perhaps tomorrow, I will take you all into the city."

"Oh, good!" cried Timothy, "I'm dying to see all of Johannesburg."

Their aunt laughed, "Johannesburg is a very big place," she said, "it would take a long time for you to see all of it."

In a little while Tricia was seated at the dining-room table with her pen and writing pad.

"I don't need to write, Tricia, if you're writing," said Timothy, "you can give my love to Mum and Dad . . . "

"Oh, no," said his sister firmly," that won't do at all. You must write a letter to them yourself, you know they will expect to hear from you. Don't be so lazy."

Timothy frowned. How he hated writing letters! Reluctantly he joined his twin at the dining-room table.

"I don't know what to say," he grumbled.

"Oh, Timothy," cried Tricia, "after our exciting journey! Tell them how the pilot took you into the cock-pit and showed you everything."

Timothy's face cleared.

"Oh, Yes," he said. Even so he sat for a while sucking the end of his pen before he began to write laboriously.

Tricia wrote easily and happily,

"Dear Mummy and Daddy,

"Uncle Dennis sent you a cable to tell you we had arrived safely, but now I must tell you all about our journey. I can't believe that it is only two days since we left home—it seems ages and ages. Timothy says that we came over five thousand miles in the plane. I hate to feel that I am so far away from you. I felt very homesick in the plane in the night when the lights were all low. But in the end I said my prayers and then I felt better. I couldn't kneel down and say them properly, but I said them in my heart and asked Jesus to help me and He did. I felt nervous at first in the plane but it was very steady. It was fun having our meals on little blue trays on our laps. The steward brought them round. The Air Hostess was very kind to us, she brought us Coca-Colas whenever we wanted them. There was a dear little baby boy on the plane and his Mummy let me sit by his play-pen and play with him for part of the time.

We came down twice in the night and had to get out while they put more petrol in the plane. Timothy knows the names of the places, as he wrote them all down in his book, and the countries we went over.

It was very exciting when we came down at Johannesburg. Crowds of people were waiting there to meet our plane and we wondered which would be Uncle and Auntie. Then a big man came out and spoke to the Air Hostess, and it was Uncle Dennis. Auntie Betty and Gina were inside. Her real name is Georgina but they call her Gina for short. She is nearly as tall as me and has very fair hair and blue eyes. She is like Uncle Dennis. Auntie Betty says I am like you, and I think that she is like you, too, and I'm glad she is because it reminds me of you. I like Auntie Betty very much. The sunshine is lovely here today and Gina says it is like this nearly every day. This afternoon she is going to take us to a lovely park right near here, and tomorrow Auntie Betty says she will take us all in to see the city. That will be exciting. I sleep in Gina's room—it is a very nice bedroom with pale green furniture. Timothy has a nice room too.

Auntie says that we are to go to school here, but it is holidays this week. It starts again next Tuesday. Auntie says I need not go till I feel well enough and want to, but I think I would like to go with Gina. Timothy can go with the boy next door. There is a dog here named 'Patch' because he is white with a black patch over one ear. He is very friendly, and if you throw his ball for him he loves you very much.

"I miss you so much, Mummy. I didn't cough very much on the plane, but I did when we first came down. It's a horrid feeling when the plane is coming down, you have to fasten the belt round you.

Please give a kiss to Melanie and to Brian from me.

Lots of love and hugs and kisses to you. Please write soon, Mummy. it will be thrilling to get a letter from you.

Your loving Tricia."

Timothy's epistle was brief and to the point.

"Dear Mum and Dad,

"It was super on the Comet. I think flying is great fun.

The pilot was very decent and took me into the cockpit and showed me all the dials and things he works. I want to be a pilot when I grow up. We came down at Rome and Khartoum and Nairobi (where we had a whopping big breakfast), and Salisbury and then Johannesburg. All these places were in different countries and I wrote the names down in my book. It's very hot here because it's summer, we don't need our coats. Uncle Dennis is very big, I like him and Auntie Betty too.

Much love from Timothy."

The twins and Gina spent a happy afternoon exploring the Park where they met several of Gina's friends. Tricia was very interested watching the small children playing on the grassy lawns with African nannies in charge of them. The latter were talking loudly and laughing together while they each kept an eye on their respective charges. Tricia was fascinated as she listened, for the language they were speaking sounded so funny.

"It's Zulu," said Gina, "and it's got clicks in it. Daddy can speak it, too, he can speak three languages," she said with pride, "English and Afrikaans and Zulu."

Timothy found his way along to the swimming pool and wished that he could join the youngsters who were having such fun, for he was very keen indeed on swimming.

That evening he asked his uncle, "When can I go swimming at the Park, Uncle?"

"Let me see," said Uncle Dennis, "today is Friday. Tomorrow you are going into the city with Aunt Betty in the morning. But in the afternoon, we can go for a swim if you like. Are you keen on it?"

"Yes, Uncle, very keen," answered Timothy.

"He's won some prizes for swimming in the Baths at home," said Tricia.

"Aw! they're nothing," said Timothy, looking uncomfortable, "but I'd love to go swimming tomorrow with you Uncle."

At bedtime that evening, Auntie Betty asked the twins, "And how has your first day in South Africa gone?"

"It's been lovely, Auntie, thank you," said Tricia shyly.

"It's super here," was Timothy's verdict, "I think I'm going to like South Africa very much.

CHAPTER VII

SATURDAY

THE next morning Auntie Betty and the three children went into Johannesburg city on the trolley bus. They managed to get the front seat on the top deck so that the twins had a splendid view of everything that was to be seen. When the city itself came into sight, Timothy exclaimed, "Oh, what high buildings!"

"Yes," said his aunt, "we have quite a lot of skyscrapers in our city, though they are not so high as those in America of course."

"And look at all the cars," cried Tricia, "I've never seen so many cars all at once. Daddy was saving up to buy a car for us, but now he's had to use the money for our fares out here."

"It does cost a lot of money to travel by air," said Auntie Betty, "but I'm sure it's going to be well worth while. Here we are at the terminus, we get out here."

Down they clambered. Tricia clung to her auntie's hand.

"What crowds of people!" she said, and, indeed, they were in danger of being separated by the people who jostled them on the crowded pavement.

"Saturday morning is always a very busy time in town," explained her aunt, "come, we'll go into Barton's."

They turned into one of the largest departmental stores in the city.

"We've got big shops like this in Liverpool," said Timothy.

"But this one's got more things in it," remarked Tricia.

It was true, such an inviting array of goods was spread out everywhere that Auntie Betty kept losing the children as they stayed behind to admire this and that.

"I tell you what," said their Aunt, "I'll leave you three in the toy department while I go and do my less interesting shopping, but don't go anywhere else."

Off went Auntie Betty to the household department, and what an interesting time the children had till she came back. Tricia fell in love with a sewing and embroidery set, for she was very clever with her fingers. Timothy concentrated on the latest models of cars and lorries and cranes and tractors, while Gina, who was a great reader, browsed among the books. All too soon, Aunt Betty was back, and said, "Let's go up in the lift to the restaurant and have some coffee."

"Whoop!" said the lift which was packed to capacity, as it took off for the fourth floor.

Auntie Betty had her coffee, but the children chose cold drinks for it was a hot day. Tricia and Gina chose milk shakes with a raspberry flavour, but Timothy had an ice cream soda, and a plate of exciting cakes was brought from which they each selected the one of their choice.

"What's that big building?" asked Timothy, when they came out again to the main street.

"That's the City Hall, and behind it is the Public Library. There are some lovely gardens between, and we will walk through them."

Tricia was delighted with the gay flowers in the gardens, and the green, well-kept lawns, and especially with the fish-pond and its little fountain in the middle which shot a dainty spray of water over the leaves of the water lilies.

Timothy amused himself picking out the various models of big American cars that were passing by all the time. He noticed that most of them had T.J. on their number plates.

"T means Transvaal," Gina explained, "and J is for Johannesburg."

"And what about these with T.P.?" asked Timothy.

"They are from Pretoria," said Aunt Betty, "it is only thirty-six miles from here."

"You must see our lovely new General Post Office," said their Aunt as they approached a big grey building and turned in at the main entrance, "we are very proud of it."

And indeed the twins agreed that it was a building to be proud of as they walked round admiring the paintings on the walls and the fine spacious, well-arranged, post office.

"You see," Auntie explained to the twins, "the paintings show the various ways that mail has been carried right from the earliest days in South Africa. See the early mail-runners, then the old-fashioned mail coaches, then the mail trains, and now the fast jet planes that carry letters to Britain in two days."

After their Aunt had stood in a queue to buy stamps and air-letters they came out and the next place of interest was the station.

"Oh, Mummy," said Gina, "we must show the twins the fish-pond inside the entrance."

They went into a courtyard which was green with palm trees and ferns and in the centre was a fascinating pond full of lively goldfish, all giving such a cool refreshing effect on this hot day. Tricia was enchanted with it all, but Timothy said, "Where are the trains if this is the station?"

"You have to go down these stairs to get to the platforms," Auntie explained, "only the booking hall and waiting rooms and refreshment rooms are up here. But we haven't time to go down now, we will come again and see it all, and the new station which they are building."

When they reached the bus terminus they found that a long queue was already waiting for their bus and they had to take their places at the end of it. But empty buses came along and in no time they found themselves on the top deck once more prepared to enjoy the ride home.

A lovely smell of dinner cooking greeted them when they arrived home for Jeremiah had dinner all ready, and Uncle Dennis came in a few minutes later.

"And what do you think of Johannesburg?" he asked the twins, once they were seated at the dinner table.

"It's a very exciting place," said Timothy, "and what a lot of cars!"

"And what a lot of people!" said Tricia.

After dinner Tricia was ordered off to lie down and rest with a book to read.

"Get your swimming things, Timothy," said Uncle Dennis, "we'll walk up to the park, and later on we'll have a swim. It's such a hot day that I expect lots of other folk will have the same idea."

"The sunshine is wonderful," said Timothy, as he ran joyfully to get his things, "and I've never been in a swimming pool that was in the open air before."

"Don't let him get too much sun today," warned Auntie Betty, "sunburn can be very painful if you have too much at first."

"I'll watch it," said Uncle Dennis and off they went.

When they came back, they all had tea in the shade of the big jacaranda tree in the garden.

"This tree will have beautiful mauvy-blue flowers on it next month," Gina told Tricia, "it's lovely then."

So the twins settled down happily with Aunt Betty and Uncle Dennis and Gina in this land of golden sunshine, and soon England began to seem a far-away place. Only the letters from Mummy and Daddy kept them in touch with home now as they revelled in all sorts of new and exciting experiences.

CHAPTER VIII

SUNDAY

THE next day, Sunday, dawned bright and fair. Tricia sang happily to herself as she dressed in her new Sunday frock under the admiring eyes of her cousin Gina.

"It's a lovely frock," said Gina, "like a party one."

"Mummy made it for me," said Tricia, and for a moment the gladness faded from her face and her bright sky of a moment before seemed to be clouded over. She was remembering those last hectic days at home and her mother busy at the machine making her new summer frocks. Suddenly an overwhelming longing for her mother came over her. She fought back the tears that came to her eyes, and bent down over her suitcase so that Gina should not see them.

It was a lovely frock for Sunday best, Mummy had said, a pale green silk one with white spots, and it suited her on account of the greeny tinge in her hazel eyes.

"But your dress is pretty too," Tricia said, when she could speak, "it's such a lovely shade of blue, it matches your eyes."

"Yes, I know," replied Gina discontentedly, "but I get tired of nearly always wearing blue. I want a pink dress but Mummy doesn't like pink on me."

So the girls chatted happily till Auntie Betty called them to breakfast. At the table Tricia suddenly asked Gina, "What time is Sunday School out here? At home we have it in the afternoon."

Gina looked up in surprise. "I believe it's in the morning," she said, "but I never go to Sunday School.'

It was Tricia's turn to be surprised now.

"Not go to Sunday School!" she exclaimed, "how . . . how . . . I mean" she continued, suddenly feeling embarrassed, "it would be funny to us not to go to Sunday School, wouldn't it, Timothy?"

"Rather," said Timothy.

The twins looked at Auntie Betty who suddenly felt very uncomfortable. Memories came flooding back to her of her own childhood in England when she and the twins' mother set off Sunday after Sunday to Sunday School, and the happy times they had had there.

"It's . . . it's a bit different out here in South Africa," she explained to the twins. "We have such lovely weather most of the time and Sunday is a great day for going out for picnics and for visiting friends and relations. Your Uncle Dennis likes to sleep late on Sundays, (he had not yet made an appearance) and then to get out and relax after the week's work."

But even as she spoke, she was conscious that her explanation must sound feeble to these children who had evidently been brought up to go regularly to Sunday School. She went on, "If you and Timothy would like to go to Sunday School I'm sure it will be all right, and we can go out afterwards. I'll speak to Jan the boy next door, he goes to the Baptist Church Sunday School in the next street. I expect he has gone already, today, but we can arrange for him to take you along with him next Sunday."

"Oh, thank you, Auntie," said Timothy, "we'd like to go."

"And me?" asked Gina. "If Tricia goes, I wouldn't mind going with her."

"Yes, of course, you can go if you want to," said her mother, "but when I suggested Sunday School for you before, you did not want to go."

"But it's different now if I can go with Tricia," explained Gina.

"Daddy was thinking of taking us all to Pretoria today to see the jacarandas, we hear that they are out in flower already and are, as always, a wonderful sight. They come out earlier in Pretoria than here."

"Oh, that'll be lovely, Mummy," cried Gina, "will we take a picnic lunch?"

"Yes, and you two girls can help me now to get things ready." Soon they were busy cutting sandwiches and packing the big lunch-basket.

"Don't you go to church either?" Tricia asked Gina in a whisper as they spread butter on the slices of bread that Auntie Betty had cut.

"Not in the mornings, but we quite often go in the evenings," Gina whispered back, "perhaps we'll go to-night."

"That will be nice," said Tricia looking relieved.

Soon they were out on the big highway between Johannesburg and Pretoria, speeding along at a good rate.

"Uncle Dennis drives fast," said Timothy with great satisfaction as he watched the hand of the speedometer creep up to sixty, then seventy.

"Much too fast for my liking sometimes," said their Aunt. The gum trees which lined the road in places filled the air with a sharp fragrance. To the twins the blueness of the sky above them was wonderful and the bright sunshine gave them a real holiday feeling.

As they drew near to Pretoria, they turned aside into a cool shady wooded place where many other people were already established in little picnic parties.

"This place is called the Fountains," Auntie Betty told them. "See, there is a little river flowing through it."

"And ducks on it," exclaimed Tricia joyfully.

As soon as they had decided on a suitable spot and were out of the car, the two girls ran to look at the ducks, especially one mother duck with a family of ducklings fussing round her.

Timothy went off with Uncle Dennis to explore, and Auntie Betty busied herself spreading a ground sheet and rug and unpacking the lunch basket.

By the time the others came back all was ready and soon they were tucking into sandwiches and cookies and fruit salad and cream, plus cold drinks for the children and coffee for the grown-ups out of a huge thermos flask.

"If anyone has any corners left unfilled, there are plenty of bananas here to finish up with," said Auntie Betty. But Timothy was the only one who managed to eat one, for the abundance of fruit like bananas and oranges and pineapples was proving a big treat to the children who had come from England.

"It's been a lovely picnic, Auntie," said Tricia, as they packed up the remnants afterwards.

"Rather!" said Timothy, "a super one!" But both of the twins had a niggling feeling of uneasiness when they remembered that it was Sunday. As though reading their thoughts, their Aunt said, "We will go into Pretoria now, and then get home in good time to have supper and go to church this evening, if Tricia is not too tired."

"I won't be, Auntie," Tricia assured her.

In Pretoria they drove along the avenues admiring the beautiful Jacaranda trees in full flower. The wind had blown some of the blossom down on the streets.

"It looks like a beautiful blue carpet," exclaimed Tricia, who was delighted with the beauty of the place, not only the tree-lined avenues, but the fine buildings and the charming gardens everywhere.

"Pretoria is the administrative capital of South Africa," Uncle Dennis told the twins. "We will take you up to see the Union Buildings where the Prime Minister and the other Cabinet ministers have their offices and where many other government servants work. They are very fine buildings designed by Sir Herbert Baker."

From the front of the Union Buildings, they had a

wonderful sweeping view of the whole of Pretoria and the countryside beyond. And immediately beneath them lay the famous Gardens full of lovely flowers. The canna lilies were in flower, pale pink ones, deep red ones, and pure white ones. Tricia thought she had never seen such a display of magnificient blooms.

"What a lot I shall have to tell Mummy in my next letter!" she exclaimed as they turned and came away from the Union Buildings, "Where's Timothy?"

Timothy had wandered off while she was admiring the flowers and had discovered the long pool which runs on the top terrace. The water-lilies were in flower there, mauve ones and yellow ones, and in and out of them darted hundreds of goldfish.

"Everywhere we go," he said, "we seem to find these lovely ponds full of goldfish and with fountains playing."

Then it was time to set out for home.

At supper-time Uncle Dennis said, "Auntie Betty can take you children to church if she wants to, but I'm much too sleepy to go."

So they had supper and then went off to the church in the next street. As Tricia sat there listening to the organ before the Service began, she felt happier than she had done all day. It had been a wonderfully exciting day, but now when, in the quiet of the church, she bowed her young heart before the Lord and worshipped Him, joy and peace filled her heart.

They sang the hymn 'At evening ere the sun was set', and Tricia was glad they chose that hymn for it was her mother's favourite. As she sang,,

Once more 'tis eventide and we
Oppresed with various ills draw near;
What if Thy form we cannot see,
We know and feel that Thou art here.

Tricia knew by faith that Jesus was right there with her.

Though her mother and father were far away now, and she was in a strange land, never had she felt Jesus to be so near and so dear to her as she did in church that evening.

After the Service was over, the minister spoke to them and the twins were introduced to him. Auntie Betty saw the superintendent of the Sunday School and arranged that the children should start going to the Sunday School the following Sunday.

That night Tricia knelt beside her bed to say her prayers as she had done each night since she arrived. Gina watched her curiously as she did so and as she read from the little brown Bible which she kept on the table beside her bed.

"Don't you say your prayers, Gina?" Tricia asked her that night.

"Yes, but I say them in bed," Gina replied, "I say a verse Mummy taught me when I was little. What verse do you say?"

"Well," explained Tricia, "I don't say any verse really . . . I . . . I just talk to the Lord Jesus and thank Him for all the nice things He gives us and ask Him to forgive me when I've been cross and done wrong, and to help me to be good."

Gina looked surprised.

"You talk to Him just as if He was a person," she said, "but He's far away in Heaven."

"Yes, but He's near to us too," said Tricia earnestly, "and He is a Person. He's just as near to me as you are and He sees us all the time and hears what we say."

Gina looked incredulous and a bit uncomfortable.

"I don't talk to Him like that," she said.

"Oh," said Tricia, "aren't you a Christian?"

"Of course I am," replied Gina laughing, "I'm not a heathen and I'm not a Jew so I must be a Christian.'

"Oh, but I mean giving your heart to Jesus and . . . and belonging to Him," said Tricia.

Gina looked doubtful.

"I trusted in Jesus in Sunday School at home," said Tricia, "it was a year ago, a little while after Timothy did."

"Do you mean it's something that you do?" asked Gina.

"Well, you see," explained Tricia, "it's really Jesus who's done it all for us when He died for us on the Cross, and we only have to say 'Thank you' to Him and to ask Him to forgive our sins and help us to follow Him truly."

Gina did not answer. This was all new to her and she didn't understand, but she began to think about these things now and sometimes Tricia read out to her some of the Scripture Union verses which she read each day and tried to explain what they meant.

CHAPTER IX

CHRISTMAS

TRICIA was taken to see a specialist in Johannesburg during the following week. He told her Aunt that the climate of South Africa would help her a lot. He gave permission for her to go to school, but said that she must not do any strenuous form of sport or get overtired.

"Plenty of sleep and plenty of good food including lots of ice-cream," was what he ordered, "and let her be out of doors as much as possible," he added.

Tricia thought he was a very nice doctor to order her to have ice-cream, for she was very fond of it. Another thing that she was pleased about was that he said she could stop taking the cough-mixture which she had been taking for a long time and which she disliked very much.

"Come and see me again in a month's time," said the specialist when the interview was over, "and see how fat you can get between now and then."

Gina was delighted to have Tricia to go to school with her each day now, and the two girls soon became fast friends.

"It's like having a sister," said Gina, "because we do everything together."

Tricia was in a class which was one higher than Gina's. She soon settled down and found the school life very interesting. Some things were quite different from her school in England, and she did not have so much homework to do. Also they were out of doors much more than was possible in the English weather.

In November the School Sports were held and that was a great day. Although Tricia could not join in them herself she followed each event with the liveliest interest, and cheered and shouted as loudly as the rest of the girls. When Gina won a little silver cup for being first in the high jump event, Tricia was as delighted as if she had won it herself, and led the clapping when Gina went up to receive it.

Timothy went to school each day with Jan the boy next door, and took a great liking for him. He was just about a year older than Timothy. They went to Sunday School together too. On the first Sunday as the two boys walked to the church, Timothy said, "I'm so glad that we can go to Sunday School with you, it was funny last week not to go."

Jan looked at Timothy in surprise.

"Do you mean to say that you like going to Sunday School? he asked.

"Of course," said Timothy, "we always went at home in England. Ever since I can remember, we have gone to Sunday School every week and we like it."

"So have I," said Jan, "but only because my father makes me go. I give it the miss whenever I can, but if my father finds out there is trouble. But as for liking it . . . not me!"

"My teacher at home was such a jolly person and he told us thrilling yarns from the Bible. It was fun, too, the competitions we had and winning prizes and things," said Timothy.

"The teacher here doesn't make the Bible stories sound thrilling, I can assure you," said Jan. "I'm always thankful when Sunday School is over. But I've got several prizes for good attendance."

"Do you go to church afterwards?" asked Timothy.

"Not if I can help it, man," said Jan. "But I usually have to go with Mum and Dad in the evenings, but not often in the morning, mercifully."

Timothy was silent as he thought this over. It was a new idea to him. He had always enjoyed both church and

Sunday School at home, and a year previously, he had taken the step of personally trusting in Christ for salvation. Impulsively now he confided in Jan, "When I was ten I got saved; it was when we were on our holidays at a Beach Service."

"Got saved!" exclaimed Jan, "Don't let the other fellows hear you talking about 'getting saved' or they will think you're a sissy."

"Why, what do you call getting saved out here?" asked Timothy.

"We don't call it anything, it isn't done to talk about things like that, man," Jan added firmly.

Timothy subsided into silence and just then they arrived at the church. Tricia and Gina joined them and they all went in together to Sunday School. It was a novel experience for Gina and she would have been very shy if Tricia had not been with her. They were both put in the same class. Their teacher was a Miss Fagan, and she won their hearts right away by the warm welcome she gave the children and also because she was very pretty and quite young. Soon they were vying with the other girls for the privilege of carrying her books and in bringing her little presents of flowers. In class she captured their attention by the winsome way she talked to them about Jesus. She used fascinating flannelgraph pictures to illustrate the lessons, and the two little girls looked forward to their Sunday School class each week.

Time passed quickly now for the twins and they found their new life in South Africa very interesting. And then the end of term drew near and the Christmas holidays arrived.

"Are we going away these holidays?" Gina asked her mother.

"Not this year," she said. "Daddy has decided to put off his holiday till July so that we can take the twins down to the coast in Natal when the weather here is cold."

Gina looked disappointed but her mother said, "We will have some nice outings nearer home these holidays and it will be fun looking forward to our seaside holiday in July."

Tricia and Timothy thought it was strange to have Christmas when the weather was so hot.

"It doesn't feel a bit Christmassy without the cold weather," they said.

All the same they enjoyed practising Christmas carols to sing at their Sunday School anniversary which came just before Christmas, and was a great occasion.

Then there was all the fun of getting or making Christmas presents for each other and of trying to keep them a secret.

"We always go for a picnic on Christmas Day," Auntie Betty told the twins. "We cook our turkey and take it with us cold."

"And what about Christmas pudding?" saked Timothy anxiously.

"We have that for supper when we come home—it's cooler then," he was told.

"Where will we go this year for our Christmas picnic?" asked Gina.

"Daddy is thinking of taking us to the Hartebeestpoort Dam," answered her mother.

"Oh, good!" cried Gina. Then turning to Tricia, she said, "That's a lovely place."

The two girls had great fun helping to make the mince-pies and to sprinkle sugar over them when they came out of the oven all golden and crisp.

On Christmas morning breakfast was a gay meal, and each person's Christmas presents were wrapped up in brightly coloured Christmas paper and piled beside his or her plate. What fun it was opening the packages and showing their presents to each other!

There were lovely presents from home for the children.

These had come a week or two earlier, but Auntie Betty had hidden them away until the great day. Tricia had been a little tearful at first as she thought of being so far away from her Mummy and Daddy at Christmas time, but with so much excitement all around her, she could not stay sad for long. As for Gina, she had never had such a lovely Christmas before, for having the twins there to share everything with made it all twice as nice.

It was wonderful how everyone seemed to get 'just what they were wanting' for a Christmas present. Jeremiah was called in from the kitchen to be given his Christmas present of a fine new shirt, and even Patch the terrier had a new tartan collar for Christmas and a specially big, juicy bone.

After breakfast Uncle Dennis said, "Let's get off for our picnic as soon as possible. We have a long way to go. Lots of other people will be going to the Dam I expect and we want to get a nice shady place near the water."

So they all helped Auntie Betty to pack the big picnic basket, then they piled it and themselves and Timothy's new cricket bat and ball and Tricia and Gina's presents into the car, and away they went to the Hartebeestpoort Dam, which is set like a lovely jewel among the Magaliesburg Mountains which surround it.

It was a very hot day, but they found a lovely shady place right near the water and settled themselves in.

Uncle Dennis took the children for a ramble round in the morning. He had his field glasses and he introduced the twins to several of the birds of the Transvaal which were new to them. Tricia had her bird book with her and enjoyed looking them up and finding the pictures of them.

When they got back there was just time for Uncle Dennis and Timothy to have a bathe before it was time for lunch.

How hungry they all were as they gathered round the lovely spread that was waiting for them under the trees!

Cold turkey and ham and tomatoes on picnic plates accompanied by rolls and butter. Then came the mince-pies, followed by slices of lovely golden paw-paw with lemon juice and sugar, and peaches.

"Fancy a lovely picnic like this on Christmas Day and out in the sunshine! exclaimed Tricia.

"A bit too much sunshine!" said Timothy, mopping his very red face.

But cold drinks and ice cream helped to cool them down.

"Do you ever have snow in this country?" asked Timothy.

"Yes," said Uncle Dennis, "there is often snow on the high Drakensberg Mountains, and we have had snow in Johannesburg, but not for some years now."

"I've never seen snow," said Gina.

"Snow's great fun," Timothy told her, "at home we build snowmen and pelt each other with snowballs."

For a moment he felt regret at the strange, hot Christmas which was so new to them, but the feeling didn't last long.

Snow's not very nice when it's melting and turning to slush," said Auntie Betty.

When it was cooler they played cricket and other games, and the sun was getting quite low in the western sky by the time they packed up and set out for home. The sunset sky was beautiful as they saw it between the gum trees on their homeward way. Tricia especially was delighted with its beauty.

"Tomorrow," she said, "I'm going to write and tell Mummy all about today."

"It's been a lovely, lovely Christmas," she told her Aunt as she hugged her that night when Auntie Betty was tucking up the two girls.

"It's nice getting presents, isn't it?" said Gina happily.

"Yes," Tricia agreed, "and my Sunday School teacher

at home told us that Christmas means that God gave the most wonderful present of all to us, He gave us Jesus to be our Saviour."

"That's quite right, darling," said Auntie Betty.

"But she said," went on Tricia, "that we each have to accept God's present for ourselves or it's no good."

As Auntie Betty put the light out and went back to the sitting-room, she was remembering the day long ago when she had done that, but somehow she had lost the joy that she had then. A longing came creeping into her heart for the blessing and spiritual joy that she had once known.

"Bless the child!" she said to herself as she thought of Tricia's simple faith in God, and in her heart she thanked God afresh for the Gift of His Son.

CHAPTER X

TRICIA'S LETTER

"DEAR Mummy and Daddy," (wrote Tricia the next day),

"We had a lovely time yesterday on Christmas Day, but it didn't feel at all Christmassy like it does at home, because the weather here was so hot. Did you have snow at home this Christmas? We were telling Gina what fun we have when it snows, she has never seen snow.

We went for a picnic to a place where there is a big lake. It was nice and cool by the water and we had cold turkey and ham and mincepies and Christmas cake, it was a lovely lunch. We didn't have the Christmas pudding till the evening at supper time.

Thank you for your nice Christmas present. I have never seen such a lovely painting and drawing outfit, I'm looking forward to using it. Timothy was thrilled with his present, too, and Auntie and Uncle gave him a new cricket bat. We played a game of cricket yesterday in the afternoon—of course Timothy made the most runs.

Last week Auntie Betty took me to see the doctor in the city and what do you think? I've put on five pounds in weight since I first went to him. He was very pleased and he said that I'm not a 'Janie' any more. You see he called me a 'Janie' the first time I went to him because I was so thin. He said I was like the lady skeleton that they had when he was learning to be a doctor and they named her Janie. They had a man skeleton, too, to learn the names of the bones on and they called him Jimmy. He said that when I have gained ten pounds altogether he will give me a nice box of chocolates. He is a very nice doctor. He said that if I get any browner 'my own mother won't know me'. Isn't he funny! That's because I'm sunburnt, but Timothy is browner than me.

Gina isn't a Christian, she didn't know about it. She kneels down now to say her prayers. She didn't use to. We read the Scripture Union portion together every day from my Bible, but Gina's Mummy gave her a nice Bible for Christmas. It's a blue one and it has pictures in it, so now she will be able to read out of her own Bible. We both love our teacher at Sunday School, her name is Miss Fagan. She is very pretty and she tells us lovely Bible stories. Gina and I are going for the competition to see who can say the most texts without making a mistake. We help each other to learn them. I think that Gina will win the prize because she's got a better memory than I have.

I don't see so much of Timothy now because he's always with Jan the boy next door. They are great friends and they go off together. Next week they are going climbing up a very high hill, Timothy is very excited about it. He's so afraid it will rain that day. The rain out here is very heavy, it just pours and pours sometimes, then it stops and the sun comes out and soon everything is dry again. All the winter here it doesn't rain at all, they say, but it's the wet season now.

My cough is much better and some days I don't cough at all except when I first wake up in the morning. The doctor says it will soon stop all together and that I must stay here till it does.

Gina says that they usually go away for a holiday during the Christmas break from school. But this year Uncle Dennis is putting off his holiday till July so that they can take us down to the seaside in Natal. Auntie Betty says it is very cold here in July but it's warm in Natal. It will be very exciting to go there but it's not for six months yet.

This is a long letter but I had such a lot of things to tell you. Auntie Betty says that if I write much more I won't be able to get the letter into the air-mail envelope so I'd better stop. She sends her love to you and so does Gina. Timothy will be writing to thank you for your Christmas present (I hope), but he sends his love meantime, Please give Melanie and Brian a big kiss from me.

Lots of love and kisses to you and Daddy

from Tricia."

P.S. I had quite a good report from school. I like the school here very much. I don't go into the Afrikaans classes, the teacher said it wasn't worth it but I've learnt quite a lot of Afrikaans words. The Afrikaans girls in our class are very nice. I always say 'Totsiens' to them when we come out of school. That means 'Till I see you again',—like 'Au Revoir' in French.

We don't start school again till January 15th. I expect we'll have lots of fun these holidays."

CHAPTER XI

CLIMBING ADVENTURE

IT was true what Tricia had said in her letter home that Timothy and Jan were almost inseparable now. Timothy looked up to the tall fair Afrikaans boy and thought he was wonderful and was prepared to follow him anywhere. And when Jan had invited him to climb one of the foothills in the Magaliesburg range, he was overjoyed. He ran to ask permission from his Aunt and Uncle.

"Jan's father is going to take us to the foot of it early in the morning and he will come and meet us there again just after sunset."

"It should be all right," Uncle Dennis told Auntie Betty, "it's not a very difficult climb except for the krantz (rocky projection) at the top and they would not go up that. But you must be back at the foot of the mountain before dark," he told Timothy, "be sure and tell Jan that."

"Yes, I will," agreed Timothy eagerly, "and Auntie, can I have some lunch to take with me. Jan wants to leave as soon as it's light."

So Auntie Betty packed up a generous supply of sandwiches and cake and fruit and put in a bottle of ready-to-drink lemonade and two bottles of coco-cola. This was packed into Timothy's knapsack the evening before together with his mackintosh.

"I'll leave a thermos of hot coffee for you on the kitchen table," Auntie Betty told him, "and some bread and butter and hard-boiled eggs. Make a good breakfast before you go."

"Oh, thank you, Auntie," said Timothy gratefully.

So it came to pass on the day planned the two boys crept out of their homes in the grey light of dawn and Jan's father drove them twenty miles to the foot of the mountain they wanted to climb. They got out of the car and looked up at it.

"It doesn't look terribly high," said Timothy, "does it?"

"You'll have done a stiff day's walk if you get to the top of that and back by sunset," said Jan's father.

"Have you got your watch, Jan?" he asked.

"Yes, Dad," replied Jan.

"Then be sure to be back here by seven o'clock at the latest," said his father. "I will wait for you just here. Totsiens (Goodbye), and 'Good climbing'."

"Totsiens," said the two boys together.

The car drove off and Jan and Timothy adjusted their knapsacks on their backs and set off on their climb.

It was a fine morning in spite of all Timothy's fears, fresh and lovely. The early morning dew was still sparkling on the tips of the long grass and on the bushes amongst which they wended their way. There was only a footpath and at first it was quite easy going.

Timothy was in high spirits. He fingered lovingly the fine scout knife which Tricia had given him for Christmas and which he was wearing hanging on his leather belt. He felt it was good to be alive on such a morning and off for a day's outing with Jan.

"Swartkop is the name of this peak," Jan told Timothy, "you know what that means, don't you?

"Well, let me see," said Timothy, "in Afrikaans 'swart' means 'black' and 'kop' means 'head', so it must be 'black cap' I suppose."

"That's right," said Jan, "because the rocky outcrop at the top of the peak is so black."

At first the path lay through woods and it was very pleasant walking. But later the path came out into the open and became more steep. Now there were only scrubby bushes, no more trees to give them shade. They started to climb in real earnest.

Timothy was singing to himself in his clear young voice,

If God be for us, if God be for us,
If God be for us, who can be against us?
Who? Who? Who?
Who can be against us, against us?

It was a new chorus which they had learned recently in Sunday School. Jan laughed as he said to him, "You'll soon need all your breath for climbing without wasting it on singing," Then he added, "You're a funny kid, Tim, aren't you? You always talk about God as though He were a real Person to you."

"So He is," said Timothy, "since I believed in Him."

"He doesn't seem real to me," said Jan, "He seems like some far-off Spirit that you go to church to worship, but nothing to do with everyday life."

"That's because you don't know Him," said Timothy. "You see, it's really through Jesus that we can get to know Him; when we trust in Him, He makes God seem real to us, and He's our Father then. It's a jolly nice feeling having God for your Father and knowing Jesus as your Saviour and Friend. I do wish I could explain about it properly to you."

"Oh, don't worry, man," said Jan, "I'm not worrying." They trudged on in silence for a while, concentrating on the rather steep part of the hill that they were on just then. The sun was very hot indeed now and they stopped from time to time to mop their faces and necks and to shift their knapsacks to a more comfortable position.

They were glad when, a little later on, the path ran into a sort of gully on the hillside through which a small stream burbled and tinkled its way down. By the side of this there were one or two trees, and the boys decided to have a short rest here and some refreshments, for it seemed a very long time ago since they had breakfast and they were both hungry and thirsty.

Thankfully they removed their haversacks and sat down in a shady spot by the stream. Out came their lunch boxes and soon they were tucking in. Jan had some special pasties which he put down between them.

"Help yourself," he said to Timothy, "Mum's pasties are pretty good."

"Mhm!" I should say they are," said Timothy, after he had sampled one. "And these cookies that Auntie Betty made are super," he said, "try one."

"I'm not going to eat as much as I'd like to," said Jan, "because the stiffest part of the climb is before us; we'll have another feast when we get to the top."

Timothy drank some lemonade, but Jan had a bottle of cold coffee. They packed everything back into their haversacks, then Jan said, "Dad lent me his field-glasses, let's have a look at the country below us."

The boys got up and walked to the edge of the hill from whence they had a wonderful view of the landscape for many miles. They took it in turns to look at it through the glasses, till Jan said, "Come, we'd better push on and get to the top."

"What's the time?" asked Timothy.

"It's half-past one," said Jan consulting the watch which had been his Christmas present from his parents, and of which he was very proud. "It'll take us all our time to get to the top and right down again by sunset."

"It'll be easy enough going down, I should think," said Timothy.

Feeling greatly refreshed by the break, they got going again with fresh energy. After a while, the path faded out and they just had to pick their way from rock to rock, Jan sometimes giving Timothy a haul up some of the steeper ones. Timothy found the going hard, but he wouldn't admit it, and though his heart was thumping loudly in his ears, and at times he panted for breath, he kept on till at last they reached a flat place at the top.

"We've done it," said Jan triumphantly, as they flung themselves down to rest and to get their breath back.

Behind them there was still the outcrop of blackish rocks that went up another twenty feet or more, but the place where they were resting was considered the top. They had another tuck in from their food packs and a drink, and sat there for a while well-pleased with themselves.

After a while Jan turned round and had a good look at the krantz (rocky outcrop).

"My!" he said, "I'd love to climb up to the top of that."

"It looks terribly difficult and dangerous," said Timothy, who had no such ambition for his legs ached and he felt more tired than he would admit.

"I believe I could do it," said Jan. "None of the other fellows at school have done it, wouldn't it be fun to be able to crow over them!"

"I . . . I don't think I could," said Timothy unhappily.

"Of course not," said Jan, "and I shouldn't dream of letting you try anyway. But I've got spikes on my shoes—I think I'll have a shot at it."

"But won't it make us late?" objected Timothy. "What's the time now?"

"It's four o'clock nearly," said Jan, "we should manage it, it won't take long, that is if I can do it at all. "You stay here."

Timothy didn't feel at all happy as he watched his friend tackle the rocky mass.

"Don't worry," he called back to Timothy, "if I find it too hard I'll come back."

Timothy stayed with the two knapsacks anxiously watching his friend. Sometimes Jan disappeared from sight as he went round the back of some of the rocks to scale them. Once he was gone so long that Timothy was very worried. But eventually he appeared again far up almost at the top. He came to the edge and looked down and waved triumphantly to Timothy. The next moment before Timothy's horrified eyes, he lost his balance, clutched wildly at the air, then came hurtling down.

CHAPTER XII

THE RESCUE

FOR a minute Timothy stood as though paralysed, overcome with shock and horror, then he ran in the direction of the spot where Jan had fallen. Frantic with fright, he searched at the side of the rocks over which Jan had lost his balance. At first he could not see him at all, then suddenly, he spotted a crumpled heap on the ground just below a protruding rock.

"Jan, Jan," he called, as he ran and dropped on his knees beside his friend, but there was no response from Jan. Was he dead? In his panic, Timothy thought at first that he was, even while he was praying desperately out loud, "Don't let him be dead, please God, oh, don't let him be dead."

Trembling himself in every limb, Timothy bent over his friend. Jan's head had fallen back, his face was deathly white and down it some blood had started to trickle from a bad gash in his head. But, to his great relief Timothy saw that Jan was breathing. He was alive, but quite unconscious. He noticed now that his friend was lying right near the back edge of the hill top, and he shuddered as he looked over that edge and saw that the ground fell away for hundreds of feet below. Another few inches and Jan would have been over the precipice!

He took a firm hold of Jan and began gently to pull him away from the edge and towards a big overhanging rock near them. But at the first movement Jan gave a loud groan which made Timothy jump.

"Jan, Jan," he called again, it's Timothy—speak to me Jan, where are you hurt?"

But Jan's only answer was another deep groan. Then

to Timothy's horror, he started up and turned over towards the precipice edge. Timothy flung his arms round Jan, and, digging his heels into the ground, with all his strength, he pulled him back and right up closer to the over-hanging rock. He was panting with the exertion by the time he got him there, and as for Jan the sweat was running down his face and it was clear that he was in great pain. He opened his eyes and looked wildly round, then gradually he focussed them on Timothy's face.

"Tim," he said, and oh, how thankful Timothy was to hear his name!

Jan groaned and put his hand up to his head. But when he spoke again, it was to say, "My leg! I think it's broken."

Timothy thought so, too, when he had looked at it and had seen the funny angle at which it was sticking out.

"Oh, Jan," said Timothy, "I'm so glad you are alive, I . . . I thought at first you were dead. I had to pull you away from the edge—I was so afraid you would go over. Oh, dear, what can I do to help you?"

He pulled out his handkerchief and wiped the blood and sweat from Jan's face. After a minute Jan said, "There's a small First Aid kit in my knapsack, man, bring it here." Timothy ran back and brought both of their bags. He opened Jan's and took out the First Aid box.

"Take a cottonwool swab and a gauze dressing and put it on this cut in my head and press hard on it to stop the bleeding," panted Jan with difficulty.

Timothy did as he was told and after a few moments the blood stopped running down Jan's face, though the dressing was soaked.

"Now put a clean dressing on and tie it tight with one of those bandages," Jan told him.

Timothy's face was white at the sight of so much blood, but he applied the clean dressing and with a groan, Jan lifted his head as Timothy wound the bandage round and round it.

"Tight," said Jan, "pull it tighter."

When it was done, Jan lay back exhausted and groaning. "My leg's the worst," he said.

After a while he raised his head and looked down at his injured leg. "Help!" he exclaimed, as he saw the unnatural angle of it, and his face went even whiter than it had been before. Then he said, "Tim, try to put my leg straight in a line, will you?"

"But it'll hurt you, Jan," said Timothy.

"Never mind about that," said Jan, "it'll ease the pain in the end—try man, quick."

Reluctantly Timothy took the broken leg gingerly in his hands and tried to straighten it. It looked more natural when he had done it but Jan had fainted right away.

Timothy looked round for some water but there was none. So he took the cold lemonade from his bag and poured some of that over Jan's face to try and bring him round. Jan gave a gasp and opened his eyes again. He licked the lemonade round his lips then gave a wry smile.

"That tasted good," he whispered.

Timothy held a mug of lemonade to his lips and he drank thirstily.

"My leg's easier now," Jan said, after a little silence, "thanks, man." He closed his eyes and seemed as though he was going to sleep.

Timothy looked round and saw that the sky had clouded over. He walked to the edge and looked out.

"Oh, dear," he said to Jan on his return, "I'm afraid it's going to rain. What shall we do? Shall I go down for help? But I don't like to leave you all alone."

"I'm all right," said Jan, "what's the time by my watch?"

"It's half-past five," said Timothy, after peering at the

watch in the failing light, for thick dark clouds had covered the sky.

"You could get down the hill in an hour and a half if you hurried," said Jan, "and Dad will be there at seven and you could tell him."

But just then Timothy noticed that wisps of white mist were rolling around the hill top and when he went to look he found that the whole place was rapidly becoming enveloped in mist.

"That settles it," said Jan, when he told him, "you can't go now. We'll just have to stay here and when Dad finds that we are not there, he'll organise a search party and they'll come up and find us eventually. I'm getting cold," he added, "my jersey is in the pack."

Timothy helped Jan into his jersey, then he put his own on. He settled himself as comfortably as possible with his back to the rock. Then he eased Jan's head on to his lap and covered them both with their two mackintoshes. They sat in silence for a while, Timothy busy with his own thoughts and Jan concentrating on trying to bear the pain he was in without groaning.

"How's the pain now?" Timothy asked after a little while.

"It's . . . it's there," said Jan through white lips.

"I saw some aspirin in the First Aid box," said Timothy, "wouldn't they help?"

"That's an idea," said Jan, "give me a couple." He gulped the aspirin down with the cold coffee that was left, and they relapsed again into silence.

After a while Timothy said, "Jan, I've just been thinking how good God has been to us—I mean, you might have fallen on to a rock instead of the ground here and then you would have been hurt worse."

"I'd have been killed outright then I expect," said Jan.

"Oh, Jan!" whispered Timothy, and Jan felt the shudder which ran through the body of his friend, "and you wouldn't have been . . . have been . . . ready."

Jan knew what he meant, but he didn't reply.

It was quite dark now and getting very cold. Both boys were shivering.

"If I could find some twigs or wood," said Timothy, "I could make a small fire." He jumped up, and covering Jan carefully, he started to search around with his torch.

"Be careful not to go near the edge," warned Jan.

Cautiously Timothy crept around and found a few twigs and some dry grass. He broke off some wood from the small bushes he found. He had seen matches in Jan's sack. He got these now and soon had a small fire going. He protected this by putting some big stones round it.

"That's grand," said Jan between chattering teeth, as he held out his frozen fingers to the blaze.

"Tim," he said, "you must eat the food that's left—you must be starving . . . I . . . .I don't want any."

"I'm not hungry," said Timothy, and indeed he felt so shaken by what he had been through in the last two hours that the thought of food made him feel sick.

"Is there anything left to drink?" asked Jan, "I'm thirsty."

"Yes, there's two Coca-Colas," said Timothy. He opened them and they had one each. Then they settled down by the little fire which Timothy carefully replenished from time to time.

"Try to sleep, Tim," said Jan, "and I will too."

They closed their eyes, but neither could sleep, though they were not so frozen now.

It was in the grey dawn of early morning that Jan's quick ears heard a shout.

"They're coming," he cried. "Go, Tim, and shout from the edge."

Timothy put his hands to his mouth and shouted for all he was worth. The mist had disappeared, and very soon he saw the powerful light of a torch below, and dim figures moving behind it. He went down to meet them and found Jan's father, his Uncle Dennis, and two other men.

At the sight of them something happened to Timothy, and to his horror, he found himself choking with sobs. His uncle put his arms thankfully round the boy and held him tight for a minute. When he could speak, Timothy said, "Jan's hurt—he fell, and we think his leg is broken. Oh, uncle, I'm so glad you've come."

Jan's father hurried on to his boy followed by the others who were carrying a stretcher.

"We've got an ambulance at the foot of the hill," Timothy's uncle told him, "just in case either of you were hurt. Come, son, it's getting lighter every minute, we'll soon have you safely home."

"What about Jan?" said Timothy anxiously.

"Don't worry any more about him," said his uncle, "his Dad and the ambulance men will look after him."

They went up and collected the knapsacks. One of the ambulance men was fixing Jan's leg in a temporary splint. When he saw Timothy, Jan told his dad, "Tim's a grand chap, he did everything for me."

"Aw, No," said Timothy, "I didn't do anything."

Soon Jan was on the stretcher, and as the eastern sky lightened with dawn, the little procession set off down the hill.

What a welcome was waiting for Timothy when he and Uncle Dennis arrived home! Gina was asleep, but Auntie Betty and Tricia were up and waiting for him. Tricia wept with relief when he came in and hugged her twin as though she would never let him go again.

Timothy started to tell the story of all that happened, but Auntie Betty cut him short, "Drink this hot cocoa," she said, "and into a hot bath straight away and then bed for you."

Timothy was more tired than he realised, and once

into his warm bed he relaxed with relief and fell asleep and did not wake up till midday the next day.

His first thought then was for Jan.

"He's in hospital," Auntie Betty told him, "he's had some stitches in his head, and his broken leg has been set, and the doctor says he'll be as right as rain in a few days."

"When can I see him?" asked Timothy.

"Not today," Auntie Betty replied, "perhaps tomorrow if the doctor says he may have visitors."

Actually it was four days before Timothy was allowed to visit his friend for he became really ill with threatened pneumonia.

But with injections of the wonder drugs of today, the danger passed and all was well.

The two boys greeted each other shyly, but Jan's hand gave Timothy's hand a grip which spoke volumes. They chatted till a nurse came to say Timothy must go. As he turned to leave, Jan caught his hand and pulled him down towards him.

"Say, man, you know what you said up on the top there about me not being . . . ready if I had died?"

"Mhm!" agreed Timothy, colouring up and nodding his head.

"Well, I've thought a lot about it and Tim, I wanted to tell you, I'm . . . I'm ready now."

"Come," said the nurse," you must go now, Jan's had enough for today."

Timothy squeezed his friend's hand so hard that he nearly squealed, and he went out of the hospital with a warm happy glow in his heart. He felt that all that they had been through on the hilltop was well worth while when it had had this result. His best friend was now a Christian too.

CHAPTER XIII

NATAL HOLIDAY

JAN made a good recovery and soon he was hopping around with his leg in plaster. Then the plaster was taken off and he was left with only a slight limp. One sad thing though, was that he was forbidden to play rugby in the coming winter. That was a real blow, for he was a rugby enthusiast and a promising player, but the doctor insisted that they must not take any risks with that leg till it was quite normal again.

The next few months went by very quickly. Easter came and went, and in the Easter holidays Jan and Timothy went to a C.S.S.M. camp at Henley on the river Klip where they had a wonderful time. Not only did they enjoy the swimming and boating and the games, but in the Tent talks each morning and the Campfire talks in the evenings, given by the fine young man who was the Camp Leader, they learned more of what it meant to be a follower of Jesus Christ—the joys and the responsibilities of being His disciples.

After the short Easter holidays, Gina and Tricia began to count the days till the July holidays when they were all going down to Natal for two weeks by the sea. Timothy was particularly thrilled at this prospect because it had been arranged that Jan was to go with them. Uncle Dennis had said to Auntie Betty one day, "You know, Timothy will be rather 'odd man out' on this holiday, what about inviting Jan to come with us?"

"A very good idea," agreed Auntie Betty, "will you speak to his father?"

Jan's parents were delighted for him to go as they felt

it would do him so much good. As for the two boys, when they were told they went around whooping with excitement and joy.

The weather had become cold in June, but it was a dry, crisp cold which seemed to suit Tricia very well.

"Watch out for the south wind," the doctor had warned her Aunt.

"When that blows see that she is well wrapped up, or keep her in."

He was very well pleased with the progress Tricia had made, and she had long ago earned the promised box of chocolates by gaining ten pounds in weight. She hardly ever coughed now, and revelled in the sunshine. It was a constant source of wonder to the twins that the sun continued to shine most days, even though it was now winter.

Excitement ran high as the June days passed, though at times it seemed to Gina and Tricia that the First of July would never come, for that was the day on which they were to set out for Natal.

But it came at last, and that morning the alarm clock in Auntie Betty's room went off at five o'clock, but all three children had been awake and up for some time before that. It was dark as they dressed in their new holiday clothes, the girls in gay cotton frocks and Timothy in khaki shorts and bright American singlet.

Jan, similarly clad, joined them for their early breakfast, and then they and the luggage were all packed into the car, and just before the sun popped up away on the eastern horizon, they set off on the long drive from the High Veld down to the coast of Natal.

It was very cold at first and the children were glad to snuggle down under warm travelling rugs, though they were full of high spirits, the boys teasing the girls, and all of them chattering at the pitch of their voices.

"Not so much noise," said Uncle Dennis, "until we

are past the town, or you will wake people up."

As for Auntie Betty, she was thankful to lean back in her seat and relax after the hectic days of packing and preparation for the holiday. She had been awake half the short night, too, worrying lest she had forgotten anything important. So now she felt how good it was that they were really off.

"All you have to do now, Mother," said her husband, "is to sit back and enjoy yourself, and for once in your life have a real rest."

"Where are we going to stay, Mummy?" asked Gina.

"At Scottburgh," said her mother, "at a hotel on the front. I wanted to take a cottage and for us to look after ourselves, but Daddy said that that would not be any rest for me, so we will be at the hotel and I shall not have to think about meals or anything else in the way of household duties for two whole weeks, won't that be wonderful?'

"I'm glad, Auntie," said Tricia, "that you're going to have a rest and it will be great fun staying at a hotel. Timothy and I have never stayed at a proper hotel."

"What is the hotel called?" asked Timothy.

"The Black Marlin," said Uncle Dennis, "that is the name of a fish that is sometimes caught in the waters of the Indian Ocean.

"Have you ever caught one, Daddy?" asked Gina.

"No," said her father, "but perhaps I'll be fortunate enough to do so on this holiday."

As the sun rose higher in the sky it grew warmer, and when they started to drop down from the High Veld to the lovely valleys of Natal, they all had to peel off their warm jerseys and put away the rugs.

"How lovely and green the country looks," said Auntie Betty, "after the brown Transvaal."

"Yes," said her husband, "they get rain down here even in the winter."

About mid-day they stopped at one of the picnic sites

at the side of the road, specially planned for motorists, and had a picnic lunch to which they all did justice. The children had been much too excited to eat a proper breakfast, so they were hungry now. What fun they had chasing each other round to stretch their legs after lunch was over while Auntie Betty packed up the lunch basket! Then into the car once more and off they went!

The twins were thrilled to see more of South Africa and listened with interest as Uncle Dennis pointed out to them places which had been famous in the Boer war, specially Ladysmith and Colenso and Majuba Hill.

They did not stop again till they got to Pietermaritzburg, when it was about three o'clock in the afternoon.

"This is the capital city of Natal," Uncle Dennis told them. "How about having some tea here?"

They trooped into a tearoom, and while their elders enjoyed a nice cup of tea, the children had cold drinks.

"Have you ever been in Natal before, Jan?" asked Uncle Dennis.

"Yes, I have once," replied Jan, "but we went by train and it was at night-time, so I'm most interested to see the country by daylight."

After leaving Pietermaritzburg, they dropped down, down, down towards the sea which they reached at Durban about half-past four, but they only took a brief look at Durban.

"We will come up here from Scottburgh one day and explore Durban properly," Uncle Dennis promised, "meantime we'd better hurry on to our journey's end, only another forty miles."

Down the South Coast now they went catching delightful peeps of the sea at intervals. The two girls who had been feeling sleepy woke up now and peered excitedly out of the car window at the blue waters of the Indian Ocean. They were all thankful when the car pulled up in front of a pleasant looking, big white building which had the form of a black fish over the entrance.

"Here we are!" said Uncle Dennis." You two boys can help me bring in the suitcases, but I will go in first and see what's what."

They were shown up to their bedrooms and were soon hanging out of the windows exclaiming loudly over the beautiful views of the sea, and of the lovely gardens in front of the hotel.

They were just in nice time to unpack and sort themselves out, and freshen up with a wash and change before the musical gong announced throughout the hotel that it was time for the evening meal. After that the two girls were so sleepy that they were packed off to bed, but the boys had a run down to the beach with Uncle Dennis before their turn came.

Next morning the fun started as they hurried down to the clean grassy slopes and the sands of Scottburgh beach. It was quite safe to bathe there because there were shark nets for the safety of the bathers. So the children and Uncle Dennis spent the whole morning in and out of the sea, bathing, and then sun-bathing—eating ice-creams which an Indian waiter brought round—building fine sand buildings and seeing the tide come in and wash them all away.

Auntie Betty was content to sit in a deck chair and relax. Though she had a book with her and her knitting, she did not look at either. She was far too interested watching the blue sea with its white breakers curling over in the most fascinating way. And when she wasn't watching them, it was interesting to watch the people all around them—other happy family parties. One party near to them had a terrier like Patch, and he was enjoying himself thoroughly.

"I wish we could have brought poor Patch with us," said Gina, "he'll be missing us all so much."

"Yes, I'm afraid he will," said her father, "but Jan's

father has promised to go in and take him for walks, and Jeremiah is there."

The weather was lovely. It was warm enough to wear summer clothes except for a cardigan in the evenings. All day long the sun shone out of a bright blue sky, and when they were not on the beach, they went for drives along the coast road, admiring the picturesque countryside with it's wild banana trees and palm trees, and inland the vast stretches of green sugar-cane fields fascinated them all.

One day they went over a sugar mill and saw the processes by which sugar was made. Another day they went into Durban and explored. There was so much to see on the front with the Children's Bathing Pool and the miniature railway train on which the children had a ride. They went up and looked at the fine shops, but did not linger there. After all they had good shops in Johannesburg, and the sea drew them back as a magnet draws a needle. Perhaps the highlight of that day was their visit to the Aquarium about three o'clock in the afternoon which is the time when the Indian diver goes down in the water, with oxygen in a cylinder strapped on to his back, to feed the fishes.

"But I never saw such lovely fishes," said the children over and over again. "Look at those blue ones," cried Tricia.

"And these pink ones" said Timothy," and these dear little yellow ones," added Gina.

"I like watching the huge turtles," said Jan, "see, that one is eating out of the diver's hand." The sand sharks and the sting rays, in fact all the fish, as they swam round and round in their huge circular tank fascinated the young people and it was difficult to tear them away when it was time to go back.

It was on the Sunday when they went to the little local church that they heard that Beach services for children were being held at a place a few miles down the coast. Jan and Timothy were so keen to go to this place that the next morning Uncle Dennis took them all there in the car.

They were a little late in arriving and a good crowd of children in the foreground and grown-ups in the background were already gathered. A big sand platform had been erected and on this stood a cheerful young man who was conducting the singing, and beside him a girl about fifteen-years-old accompanied the singing with her squash-box.

Timothy and Jan soon joined with the other boys present in the singing of the choruses and so did Tricia and Gina for they had learned most of them in Sunday School. A strange hush came over the beach congregation when the young man on the platform took off his hat and bowed his head and started to pray to God. Only the sound of the waves breaking on the beach broke the stillness now. Then another young man came on to the platform and soon the children were enthralled listening to him as he talked to them about Jesus, the One around whom the boys and girls of Palestine clustered long ago, and who still, today, calls boys and girls of all countries to follow Him.

The speaker did not go on for very long but he so presented Christ to the children that in the hearts of some of them there was stirred a longing to know and love this "Friend of little children'."

Auntie Betty noticed the wistful look on Gina's face as she listened, and it brought back to her memories of long ago when she had been a child and had attended such beach services in England.

Even Uncle Dennis said afterwards, "Well, that chap certainly knows how to preach to kids, I wonder who he is."

Later on they found out that he was Mr. Green, a missionary, who was home on furlough from India, and that evening they saw him at dinner in their hotel and found that he was staying there for a few days.

They were all so interested to meet him afterwards, and Timothy told him, "I was saved at a beach service in Bournemouth in England nearly two years ago."

"That's good," said their new friend. Then he turned to Gina and asked, "And what about you?"

Gina hung her head shyly and did not speak, so Tricia volunteered,

"I gave my heart to Jesus in our Sunday School at home in England."

When the preacher looked at Jan, he smiled happily and said, "It was only a few months ago that I trusted in Christ—it happened in hospital, after an accident."

"That's grand," said the missionary, "I was just about your age too when I made the great Decision, and I still remember the thrill of it."

Uncle Dennis felt a bit uncomfortable as he listened to this conversation, but in his heart there stirred for the first time a faint longing for this experience about which the others were talking so happily, a longing which increased later on till eventually he too knew the joy of God's salvation.

It was in the middle of that night that Tricia woke up to hear sniffs coming from Gina's bed. She listened for a while. There was no doubt about it, Gina was crying.

"What's the matter?" asked Tricia, jumping out of bed and going over to her cousin. "Have you got a pain?"

"Yes," sobbed Gina, putting her hand over her heart.

Thinking it was a tummy pain, Tricia said, "Shall I ask Auntie Betty for a hot water bottle for you to put on it?"

"No," sobbed Gina, "it's in my heart, I . . . I want to trust in Jesus too."

"Oh," said Tricia, understanding now, "well you can, right now, if you want to."

"Not in the middle of the night," said Gina.

"Yes, you can," said Tricia firmly. "Jesus is here with us and He can see us and hear us all the time, day or night."

Gina's months spent in Miss Fagan's Sunday School class had taught her much about Jesus the Saviour of the world, so that now when the time was ripe, it was easy for her to take the step which she now longed to do, and which made her a child of God—a follower of Jesus, the Friend of boys and girls. The two little girls knelt beside Gina's bed and prayed and Jesus Himself drew near.

Tricia kissed her cousin happily and said, "You must tell Mr. Green in the morning, he'll be so pleased." And indeed he was!

CHAPTER XIV

HOME AGAIN

WHEN the family arrived back home after their holiday, everyone remarked on how brown the children were. Jeremiah, the houseboy, and Patch, the terrier gave them a joyful welcome. Patch wore himself out jumping up first to one then to another member of the family trying to assure them in his doggy way how pleased he was to have them back.

And when Tricia went for her next visit to the specialist, he pretended not to know who this 'brown berry' was! He gave her a thorough overhaul and then sent her out to talk to the Sister in the waiting-room while he talked to Auntie Betty. He said, "There is no trace whatever of bronchial trouble with Tricia now, I think we may say that the cure is complete. When is she going back to England?"

"Well," said Mrs. De Villiers, "the twins came out in October, and we thought it would be nice if they spent a year with us."

"Hmm!" said the doctor, "I wonder. Then he went on, "You know, Mrs. De Villiers, I would be much happier if Tricia arrived back in England in August while it is still summer there. To arrive at the beginning of winter in October would not be so good for her. The change from October heat here to winter in England might undo some of the good that has been done."

"Oh, dear," said Tricia's aunt, after she had thought this over, "you mean she ought to go back in August, that's next month."

"I mean," said the doctor, "that she should go back now as soon as possible. If you like I will consult with

Dr. Macduff about this by airmail, but I think he will agree with me. Meantime will you write and tell her parents what I say, and no doubt Dr. Macduff will advise them what to do."

"Yes, I will do that, Doctor," said Auntie Betty, "but we shall miss the twins very much now."

"I'm sure you will," the doctor agreed, "but you will have the compensation of knowing that Tricia's long stay with you has been the means of restoring her to good health."

Auntie Betty told Uncle Dennis what the doctor had said, but she said nothing to the children. She wrote at once to the twin's parents and waited anxiously for their reply. The very day it came she had a phone call from the specialist.

"Mrs. De Villiers," he said, "I've had a letter from Dr. Macduff, and, as I expected, he urges that the children should be flown home as early in August as possible."

"Yes," agreed Auntie Betty sadly, "I've heard from their parents to that effect too, and they want us to arrange for the journey next week.

That evening she told the children. What a shock they all had! At first the twins were dismayed! They had had such a wonderful time in South Africa. They had grown to love their Auntie and Uncle and Gina so much, and indeed, they had grown to love South Africa with its sunshine. At first the news came as a sad shock. It was only later when they began to think about the other end of the journey, about arriving in England and seeing their mother and father and Brian and Melanie and all their friends that they began to cheer up and then to get thrilled. Indeed, their feelings were so mixed by now that they hardly knew how they felt.

Then, too, there was more exciting news in the letter from home. Auntie Betty told them that their father had decided to move from the north of England down to the south where the climate would be less severe in the winter. When they arrived in London on the plane they would be taken straight to their new home in Surrey instead of going back to Liverpool. The twins were full of speculations about their new home—what the house would be like, and what the garden was like and where they would go to school and so on.

Gina was the one who was most sadly affected by the news that her cousins were going away so soon. The months they had spent in her home had been a very joyful time for her and she could not bear to think of being left as the only child there after they had gone.

So upset was she that in the end her mother decided to let her into a secret which they had not meant to tell her till later. "Do you know what, Gina," her mother said, "next year, Daddy is going to take his long leave and we will go home to England on a visit and stay with Tricia and Timothy and the rest of the family in their new home. Won't that be something lovely to look forward to?"

Gina agreed that it certainly would, and she cheered up considerably after hearing this good news.

Sadly Auntie Betty began to make preparations for the twins' journey home and Uncle Dennis went in to the Airways office to see how soon they could get a booking. Everyone looked at him anxiously when he came home that evening.

"August 5th," he said briefly.

"That's ten days from now," said Auntie Betty. "Well," she added, "let's make the very most of those ten days."

And that was the attitude of them all, 'Let's make the most of the time that is left'.

Gina went sadly back to school without Tricia, though Tricia went along one day to say 'Goodbye' to her teacher and to the other girls in her class. She was surprised how much they had all come to mean to her in the few months that she had been there.

Auntie Betty took them into town one day to buy one or two things needed for the journey and to pay a farewell visit to the specialist. He teased Tricia as usual, but he told her that he was very pleased with her and very proud of the progress she had made.

"Goodbye, Janie," he said, "and give my love to England. I came out from there, you know, but that was a long time ago, and South Africa is my country now. I wish you could take some of our sunshine back with you, but you have had a good dose of it, and from all we hear they are having a good summer over there this year."

So one by one the twins said 'Goodbye' to the friends they had made in South Africa, and prepared to leave for England.

One day they went into town with Auntie Betty to buy little presents to take back to their mother and father and to Brian and Melanie. It took them a long time to make up their minds what to get for each one of them. Their father had kept them supplied with pocket money all the time and some of this had accumulated.

"I know what," said Tricia to Timothy, "let's buy a parting present to give to Auntie Betty and to Uncle Dennis. Timothy eagerly agreed and much earnest thought was given to the matter. In the end they decided on a pretty tablecloth for Auntie, and a walking stick with an ivory handle for Uncle, for they knew that he always used a stick when he went out walking. It was great fun getting these things home without Auntie seeing them and hiding them till the right moment for giving them. For Gina, too, Tricia bought a book as a parting present, one that she knew Gina wanted. And Timothy bought a scout knife, like the one he had had for Christmas, to give to his friend Jan as a parting present, for Jan had often admired his knife.

So the days slipped quickly by. On the last Saturday, they paid a farewell visit to the Park. The Swimming bath was not open yet as it closed for the winter.

Then came the last Sunday. Tricia wept at Sunday School when she said 'Goodbye' to her beloved Miss Fagan, but her tears soon stopped with the pleasure she felt when her teacher gave her a dear little book called 'Daily Light' which had texts from the Bible arranged in daily readings. It was a lovely surprise, and Miss Fagan had written in the fly leaf and stuck in it also a small snapshot of herself. Tricia was delighted and thanked her teacher so much, and the little book certainly became one of her greatest treasures.

At the Service that evening, the minister mentioned the fact that the twins were leaving South Africa during the week and wished them Godspeed on behalf of the members of his church.

Then came the day of departure and all was bustle and confusion—of last minute packing and trying to keep within the weight limits for their suitcases.

"It's no good," said Auntie Betty at last, "we'll just have to take some things out and post them to you by Parcel Post. And that is how they got over the difficulty in the end.

Auntie and Uncle were delighted with their parting presents from the children. They too had a little send-off present for the twins, it was an enlargement of an excellent picture in colour, of the house and the family in front of it.

"Oh, how lovely, Auntie," said Tricia, "we can get it framed at home and hang it up in our new house."

Lunch was a sad and rather hurried meal and they were to leave for the airport directly afterwards as the plane was to take off at four o'clock. The twins were too full of varying emotions to be able to eat much, and Auntie Betty did not press them for she understood how they felt.

When they arrived at the airport, it was a pleasant surprise to find all sorts of people waiting there to see them off. Some of their friends were there from Day School and from Sunday School, and to Tricia's delight Miss Fagan was there. Jan and his mother and father were there too. Timothy and Jan made solemn promises to write regularly to each other; they both felt the parting keenly. The minister from the church was there and the twins went round saying 'Goodbye' to everyone.

Although she tried hard, Tricia could not keep from shedding tears when she said 'Goodbye' to Auntie Betty and to Gina. The two girls clung to each other tearfully.

"Cheer up," said Uncle Dennis, "the time will soon pass till next year when we all come over to see you."

Then the voice over the loudspeaker was calling them to go out to the plane. This time it was a Viscount, and once more they were introduced to the Air Hostess and put in her charge. But both of them felt like well-seasoned travellers by now, and they went out with the other passengers quite confidently. At the top of the steps leading up into the plane, they turned and waved a final Farewell.

"Goodbye, dear Auntie and Uncle and Gina and Jan and everybody," they murmured, and "Goodbye, dear South Africa, Totsiens!" Then they vanished inside the plane.

The twins felt only sadness as the great plane took off and rose higher and higher. They leaned on the window to get a last glimpse of Johannesburg, the Golden City, where they had been so happy.

"Do you know what," said Timothy to Tricia as he saw the mine dumps looking golden now in the late afternoon sun, "I never went down a gold mine! Uncle was always going to take me, and then somehow he never did."

"Well," said Tricia, "it was such a rush in the end. You should have reminded him. Anyway, it's too late to do anything about it now," she added practically, perhaps we'll come to South Africa again one day and then you can go down one, I shan't ever want to, I'd be frightened."

They did not remain sad for long, because now their faces were turned towards home and Mummy and Daddy. Soon they were full of excited anticipation of their arrival in London.

"I wonder whether Brian and Melanie will come with Daddy and Mummy to the Airport to meet us," said Tricia.

"I don't expect so," replied Timothy, "they are too small."

On flew their plane—all through the dark hours of the night, over land and sea. They only came down twice on the way. When the pilot told them the next midday that the sea underneath them was the English Channel and that the land they could see was the coast of England they were thrilled! The next minute the warning lights came on telling them to fasten their seat belts for landing. Then down, down, down, they came on to one of the runways of the great London Airport.

By this time the twins could hardly contain themselves with the excitement they felt. The Air Hostess helped them to gather up their coats and belongings and escorted them from the plane till they were safely handed over to their parents.

After the first hugs and kisses were over, what exclamations there were of joy and surprise!

"But how you've grown, my darlings!" cried their mother, "and as for you, Tricia, I can hardly believe it's you. You are twice as fat as when you went away, and you look so well!"

"I'm browner than Tricia, aren't I?" asked Timothy.

"Well," said his father, "I shall say like the Irishman, "you're as brown as each other and browner!"

They all laughed and the two children skipped excitedly along beside their parents.

"Where are Brian and Melanie?" asked Tricia. "We wondered if they would come with you to the Airport."

"No, they are at home—at our new home which you haven't seen yet, but I'm sure you will love it," said Mummy.

And so they did! It was nearly dark when they finally arrived there, so they could only see the inside of the house, but the next day they explored the whole house and garden and neighbourhood and Timothy's verdict was, 'Super, absolutely super!' While Tricia pronounced the new home as 'much nicer than the old one at Liverpool'.

What a lot there was to talk about that day! And indeed for many days to come, but particularly that first whole day at home. The twins took it in turns to hold the field for they were both nearly bursting with things that they wanted to tell their parents.

And when bedtime came and her Mummy was tucking Tricia up, she asked her, "And what was the nicest thing of all that happened while you were out there in South Africa?"

"Oh, Mummy, I don't know," said Tricia, thinking deeply. "So many lovely things happened." Then she went on, "But one I shall always remember is the night at Scottburgh when Gina gave her heart to Jesus in the middle of the night."

"That certainly was a lovely happening," said her mother, "and I'm so glad that you were able to help her. As you grow older you will discover that there is no joy and thrill on earth so great as that of helping people to find the Saviour."

"And Mummy," said Tricia, "Timothy helped his friend Jan to be a Christian too."

As she picked up her little brown Bible, she said,

"Mummy, Gina and I made a pact that we'll think of each other specially every day when we are reading our Scripture Union portion, because we'll be reading in the same place."

"That's a lovely idea," said her mother, as she tucked Tricia up, and went downstairs with a heart full of thankfulness that their prayers for Tricia had been so wonderfully answered.

Her husband looked up as she came into the sitting-room.

"Well," he said, "the South African sunshine has certainly done wonders for our Tricia, and Timothy too looks as fit as a fiddle, and a very brown one at that!"

"Yes," she said, "it has indeed—the sunshine, plus the blessing of the Lord. I feel like saying with the Psalmist,

'*Bless the Lord, O my soul, and all that is within me, bless His Holy Name*!' "

Printed at the Press of the Publishers